"I used
Logan

Now it
Kathryn's mouth instinctively
reached for his, her trembling fingers
threading through the thick black silk
of his hair. A sudden overwhelming
urgency shot through her at his
answering passion.

His hands caressed the warm
shuddering contours of her body and
cupped the small swell of her breasts.
He murmured almost incoherently,
"Oh, Kathryn—*Kathryn!* Let me love
you the way you were meant to
be loved."

He had said that once before—and
then betrayed her. The words washed
over her. Then the memory of his
body entwined with Carol's came
rushing at Kathryn with a sickening
jolt. What Logan had done was
unforgivable.

"Oh God! Leave me alone!" Tears stung
her eyes.

Books by Maura McGiveny

HARLEQUIN PRESENTS
674—A GRAND ILLUSION
723—PROMISES TO KEEP

HARLEQUIN ROMANCES
2511—DUQUESA BY DEFAULT

These books may be available at your local bookseller.

For a list of all titles currently available,
send your name and address to:

Harlequin Reader Service
P.O. Box 52040, Phoenix, AZ 85072-2040
Canadian address: P.O. Box 2800, Postal Station A,
5170 Yonge St., Willowdale, Ont. M2N 5T5

MAURA MCGIVENY

promises to keep

Harlequin Books

TORONTO • NEW YORK • LONDON
AMSTERDAM • PARIS • SYDNEY • HAMBURG
STOCKHOLM • ATHENS • TOKYO • MILAN

Harlequin Presents first edition September 1984
ISBN 0-373-10723-4

Original hardcover edition published in 1984
by Mills & Boon Limited

CHAPTER ONE

THE pudgy young man drew his car to the kerb and shivered as he cut the ignition. One of these days he was going to get his heater fixed. He'd been meaning to do it for a long time now, but until today he hadn't been able to afford it. He smiled to himself and slid from behind the wheel. A stiff January wind was blowing and nearly knocked him down, but he turned up his frayed collar and battled his way across the busy intersection. Not only would he have his car heater repaired, he'd buy himself a new coat too, one of those sheepskin ones that kept out the cold as well as the wet. His smile became wider. After today he would have money for all the necessities other people took for granted, and maybe he would have enough left over to take a little trip to Tahiti or Bermuda or Jamaica.

Funny, none of his cases ever took him to exotic places like that. Just once he would like to be like the private investigators on television: a good gun battle with the bad guys and him standing there making it look easy until the police came and carted them all off to jail. He would turn to the beautiful blonde beside him and . . . And what? he asked himself. His wife would kill him if he tried anything!

He was getting too old for this dream of his. It was time he accepted the fact that he was a

second-rate private investigator whose only claim
to fame was an uncanny knack for locating
missing persons.

This case was one of the easiest, Jim Price
chuckled to himself, making his way through the
shining glass doors of the downtown office
building, the easiest and yet the most lucrative.
Logan Ramsey wanted that woman found. No
cost was too great. He'd heard through the
grapevine that the man had used dozens of
agencies trying to find her. He'd searched the
globe for years, but she was gone, vanished into
thin air.

He gave the girl at the information desk in the
lobby a wide grin. 'Good morning, Jenny. How
are you this fine morning?'

'Hi, Mr Price.' She bobbed her curly red head
in his direction. 'Haven't seen you so happy in
months.'

'The end of a case, my dear, the end of a case.
Mr Ramsey in yet?'

'Bright and early this morning before any of
the rest of us were even here yet. Margaret told
me he'd been to check on several timber sites
before he got here, too. That man must work
twenty-six hours a day!'

Not after today, Jim Price thought to himself.
'Shall I go up, then?'

'I'll ring Margaret you're on your way.'

'Thanks, Jenny.' He stepped into the elevator
and whisked his way to the top floor.

The corridor was thickly carpeted in a beige
and brown and gold tweed, blending vividly with
the rich oak panelling on the walls. The faint

clicking of a typewriter was the only sound that came to him, and all at once the thought struck him that Logan Ramsey, for all his wealth and power and position, was an unhappy man. Strange, he had never realised it before. Perhaps he had been too blinded by the thought of his wealth and all the things it could buy. But Logan Ramsey was only a man, after all. And Jim Price was intrigued by the girl he had been hired to find. She was not his mistress, if he could believe the people who knew her; she just was not the type.

Once he had located her, he saw that she kept to herself. She was shy and retiring and didn't date anyone—and he wondered about that. For more than a week he followed her everywhere and noted her comings and goings. He even pretended to be the father of a fictitious four-year-old child just to talk to her in the nursery school where she worked as an aide.

She was polite but aloof, and he couldn't imagine what connection there could be between her and Logan Ramsey. His vivid imagination drummed up all sorts of possibilities. What he wouldn't give to know . . .

'Good morning, Mr Price.' Margaret Benson's voice was cold and precise, like her. 'Mr Ramsey is waiting for you.'

She didn't move from her desk, but her chilling perfection had the power to ruffle him and by the time he closed the door to her office behind him, he had lost some of his cheerful composure.

The man he had come to see was standing with

his hands carelessly resting in the pockets of his black slacks. He had his back to the room, looking out the wide windows that stretched almost completely along two walls. The room itself was spacious, but the length and breadth of the windows overlooking the city of Vancouver made Jim Price feel slightly giddy and he despised the weak feeling in his knees. How he hated heights! And yet this was the perfect backdrop for Logan Ramsey. He perched up here as if he was lord of all he surveyed. Exactly how many acres of timberland he owned was any-body's guess, but he'd heard rumours that the acreage was measured in hundreds of thousands.

He realised he was staring, nervously probing the rigid lines of the tall man's back and shoulders, and he abruptly turned and forced himself to breathe deeply. Logan Ramsey was only a man, yet he felt inferior beside him. He ran a trembling hand across the back of his neck and cleared his throat, wishing he could sit down in one of the brown leather chairs in front of the desk.

The carpeting in here was a deep russet colour and the other two walnut-panelled walls held several small paintings that reeked of the ascetic taste of their owner. For all his wealth, Logan Ramsey was not pretentious. The office was purely functional, with only a huge desk and several chairs and a low wooden cabinet set against one wall. All the sounds of the city below were muted and unreal.

'You're early today, Price,' he said quietly without turning from his contemplation of the city. 'Sit down, won't you?' He ran a hand through his thick black hair with a premature threading of grey at the temples and loosened his tie before unbuttoning the top button of his white silk shirt. Rolling up his sleeves, he seated himself behind his desk without so much as a flicker of emotion on his stony features. 'Do you have anything to report?'

Jim Price sensed the air of defeat about him. How many times had he faced him these last few months with nothing to say? And how many men had done the same thing before him? He cleared his throat. 'Yes, sir.'

'You've *found* her?' He didn't move, but the air suddenly became charged.

'Yes, sir.'

'Where?'

It was only one word and spoken so quietly that Jim Price shuddered as if a cold finger of ice had slithered down his spine. 'She's here, sir, in Vancouver.'

Logan Ramsey was holding a pencil so tightly in his long fingers that it suddenly snapped in two. He pushed it aside on the polished surface of his desk before folding his hands together. The whitening of his knuckles belied the relaxed pose and his voice was deep with rage. 'Here in Vancouver! You've seen her? Talked to her?'

Jim cleared his throat nervously. 'Yes, sir.'

'And?'

What did he want him to say? He looked at his face to get a clue as to how he should go on, but it told him nothing. A muscle was jerking in the hard line of his jaw, but what that meant was anybody's guess. He reached in his pocket and found a slip of paper with an address on it. 'This is the apartment building where she's living,' he said quietly. 'She works as an aide in a nursery school . . .' His voice trailed off miserably.

'How long?' The words were clipped.

'Er—you mean how long has she worked there?' Logan Ramsey nodded.

Running a nervous finger along the inside of his shirt collar, Jim Price swallowed. 'Five years. Her employer is the gregarious sort, he couldn't tell me enough about what a good employee she is. The children practically idolise her.'

'There's no mistake it's Kathryn?'

'Oh no, sir, there's no mistake. She's just like the picture you gave me.' He took that from his pocket too and set it on the desk between them. 'She's thinner now, but there's no doubt it's her.' He clamped his mouth shut at the sudden tightening of Logan Ramsey's white face, and whatever else he was going to say died in his throat.

'All this time she's been right here, right under my nose, and I couldn't find her! All this time. All those other agencies searching for her.' He looked across his desk to the flushed face of this beefy young man and began to laugh. It was entirely without mirth, a strangely mournful sound in the still room. 'I promised you a bonus if you found her within six months.' He reached in his drawer and withdrew a chequebook. The strokes of his pen were bold and forceful as he wrote out a cheque for an enormous sum. He stood and handed it to him. 'One other thing before you go.'

Jim Price reluctantly looked at him, not wishing to take his eyes off the cheque. 'Yes?'

'Tell me, is she married?'

'No, sir, she doesn't have a husband. She lives alone.' He clutched the cheque and shook his head before quickly turning to the door. A lot of different people reacted in various ways to the news that he had located a missing person for them, but this was the first time he'd run across rage. 'Thank you for the cheque, sir. If I can be of service to you again, you have my number.'

Logan Ramsey didn't say anything but watched him go with a fleeting sense of unreality. He'd found her. After all this time, all these years, she was here! He turned to the window and dragged his hands through his hair, staring out at the city. Of all the places he had pictured her to be, she was here. Who would have thought it?

He groped for a chair like a blind man and sat down heavily. Trembling, he picked up the small picture that lay on his desk. 'Kathryn.' He whispered her name brokenly, gripping the picture with tortured fingers.

It was a good likeness of her, even though it was one of those that developed on the spot and tended to blur. After five years it hadn't faded. She was still as vibrant as she ever was. She stood there, smiling into the camera, but he didn't need a picture to remember her in every vivid detail. She was small and slender with bright blue eyes that held the promise of love. Her hair was black and shining and tumbled in disordered waves far down her back. He had loved to tangle his fingers

in its silky thickness. Even now, just the thought
of it had the power to drive him mad.

A fine sweat broke out on his forehead and his
breathing became laboured. She's still mine, he
thought, unconsciously crushing her picture in
his powerful clenched fist. He felt the familiar
stab of pain in his chest when he thought of the
day this picture was taken. It was the day he had
asked her to marry him, the day she had
accepted.

But he had never married her.

The day after his proposal, she was gone.
Vanished. Nothing. Not a word of goodbye.

Her sister Carol was as surprised as he that she
had left. Even her aunt didn't know where she
had gone. When Logan pounded on the old
woman's door, demanding to know, she couldn't
tell him anything except that Kathryn had
decided to leave.

Why? he wanted to know. He had a right to
know. Why? For five years he had sought but
never found the answer. Now he knew where
she was and now he would find out why she left
him.

'Mr Ramsey? Logan? Are you all right?'

He ran a dazed hand across his eyes and had
trouble focusing on his secretary. 'What?' He
shook his head and cleared his throat. 'What is it,
Margaret?'

'I buzzed you several times on the inter-
com, but you didn't answer. Are you all right?'
She stood beside him, clutching at his shirt
sleeve.

'Yes, yes, I'm all right,' he said irritably. He

straightened and dropped the crushed snapshot into a drawer and pulled himself together with difficulty. 'What did you want me for?'

'Your brother's on the line. He has a free evening before he leaves for his European tour tomorrow and wants to know if you can meet him for dinner tonight.'

'You can tell that no-good brother of mine——' Logan stopped and sighed heavily. 'Never mind, I'll talk to him myself.'

She nodded and left him, and he picked up his telephone with a sweating hand.

'Sorry to keep you waiting, Paul,' he said shortly. 'I'm pretty busy. Tonight's out of the question. I've got some unfinished business to clear up . . .'

When Kathryn left the nursery school on a wet breezy evening towards the end of January, she toyed with the idea of making a side trip downtown to window-shop. But the thought of the fast approaching first of the month and all the bills that came due then quickly put an end to that idea. That was depressing enough, without looking at things she would never be able to buy even if she saved for a whole year. With any luck, she would manage to exist all week on the ten-dollar bill in her purse. It was all that stood between her and absolute poverty.

A tiny smile curved her lips. At least I have a job with regular paydays, she thought. At least I'm able to take care of myself and not have to depend on anyone else's charity. It's a fantastic feeling to be independent, she decided, and walked with a jaunty step in the direction of home.

Soon it would be spring, the season of hope. She wouldn't let anything get her down. She'd take a long hot soak in the tub and heat up some soup, then settle down with the book she had borrowed from the library only yesterday. It would be a pleasant evening, the kind she enjoyed most.

When she turned the corner on to her block, a vague feeling of apprehension slithered down her spine. This time she wasn't imagining it. For nearly two weeks now, she had had the distinct feeling that someone was following her. And it wasn't only at home but also when she was on the playground at school. She shivered, jamming her hands in her pockets before pulling her coat closer around her and running the last few yards to her apartment building.

With her foot on the top stair, she turned abruptly and looked over her shoulder with a stern frown that was supposed to mask her fear. Whoever you are, she thought to herself, you don't scare—— But before the thought had completed itself, she found herself looking down into Logan Ramsey's implacable face.

'Hello, Kathryn,' he said softly, as if meeting her outside her building was an everyday occurrence.

Her eyes widened and her jaw dropped. Goosebumps broke out all over her and she found it difficult to breathe. He was just as she remembered him: tall and handsome, his muscular frame covered in an expensive dark trenchcoat. His black hair was stylishly longer now, with the beginnings of a distinguished grey at the temples. His face was thinner and his cheekbones more prominent, but the deep clefts at the sides of his mouth hadn't altered and the mesmerising qualities of his deep blue eyes still fascinated her even after all these years.

A sudden anguish squeezed her heart, but she fought against the sensation with all her might. It seemed to take her forever to find enough presence of mind to walk back down the few steps to where he stood. He probably expected her to bolt and run, but she wasn't going to let him have the satisfaction of seeing her do the expected thing.

'Well, well. What brings you to this neighbourhood, brother-in-law?' she said softly, thankful her voice didn't quiver. 'I don't ever remember you slumming before.'

'I came to find you.' He was matter-of-fact, quiet and firm.

A dull red crept up her neck as she tried to match his tone. 'Whatever for?'

'Let's go inside. I'd rather not discuss it on your doorstep.' He tossed his windblown hair out of his eyes and gripped her elbow.

'No!' She jerked her arm away from him. 'We don't need to go inside. Whatever you have to say can be said right here. But make it short, will you? I've got a lot of things to do.'

'I intend to take you home with me. Is that short enough?'

Her jaw started to drop, but she sank her teeth into her bottom lip and tried to hang on to her temper. 'If you need someone to fetch and carry for Carol, hire a maid. I'm no longer at her beck and call.' She turned and started up the steps again, but something came and went in his eyes and he grabbed at the thin sleeve of her coat and nearly tore the worn material.

'It isn't Carol who needs you. It's Jon.'

'Jon?'

'My son.' There was no inflection in his quiet voice and he met her wary look with eyes that turned to immovable stone.

A shaft of pain sliced through her. His son! His son and Carol's. 'No, Logan. I have a well-paying job and a home of my own. There's no room in my life for you or Carol or your son. You'll have to get someone else to play nursemaid!' She ran up the steps and nearly succeeded in slamming the door in his face, but Logan was too quick for her and he pushed it back easily, following her into the entrance hall.

'I don't want you here and you know it!'

'I'm ready to leave whenever you are.' A small smile hovered about his mouth, as if he knew it was only a matter of time before he succeeded in wearing her down.

When Kathryn saw that knowing smile, the smouldering embers of her temper flared. 'I wouldn't cross the street with you,' she said angrily, lowering her voice only when several people, obviously coming home from work, tried to squeeze past them in the tiny hallway.

He gripped her elbow, urging her up the stairs, ignoring her mutinous struggles. When they stopped outside her door, he held out his hand for her key. 'Or would you rather I asked your landlady to let me in again?'

'Again?' Her eyes flew up to his.

'I brought some groceries in earlier. I know all about you, Kathryn Marshall,' he said with a wry smile. 'Mrs Adams loves to gossip, doesn't she? You're an extremely neat housekeeper, but you're a month behind in your rent. You're next in line to lose your job at the nursery school because things are slowing down now and the enrolment is falling off. The only reason you're still there is that they pay you next to nothing. You rarely go out in the evenings—and never with a man. You can't make ends meet and your cupboards are bare. Need I go on?'

A brilliant red swept up to the roots of her hair, but she thrust her chin up defiantly. 'I won't ask you how you managed to get her to let you into my flat or to tell you such things, but I will ask to you to leave. Please!'

'Sorry—I'm not leaving. I've gone to too much trouble finding you.' Logan took her bag from her resisting fingers and tipped out the meagre contents. When he found her key he scooped everything back and handed it to her, tilting his head to an arrogant angle before quirking one black eyebrow. 'The fractious child act is beginning to bore me, Kathryn, and that's the one thing you never did before. You alone never bored me.'

She stood in the dim hallway and watched him as he swung the door open and disappeared inside without waiting for her to follow. As if he owned the place! she thought with violent anger.

But anger would get her nowhere; she would have to use tact. Ice shuddered along her nerves. How could she manage to get rid of him and still keep her dignity? She wanted to throw something at him. Why did he have to come here? One look at him and all her self-protective barriers came crashing down.

The thought crossed her mind to turn and run. There was nothing much here anyway, just two tiny rooms furnished with Mrs Adams' cast-off furniture. But how far would the ten dollars in her purse take her?

'If you're through weighing the alternatives, I've got dinner started,' Logan drawled from the doorway.

Kathryn walked stiffly past him and closed the door with a decided slam.

'Do you want to change into something more comfortable while I put the steaks under the broiler?' he asked, reaching for her coat like a perfect gentleman. 'If I remember right, you like yours medium rare.'

She only pulled her coat tighter around her with an exaggerated movement and turned to face him full of outrage. 'How dare you come in here and take over as if you own the place?'

One corner of his mouth quirked. 'Actually, I do. Own the place, that is. It's one of the projects my firm was asked to invest in recently. "Clean up the slums. Provide a healthy environment for our youth"—you know the sort of thing politicians urge in their campaigns all the time?' He flicked a quick look around the nearly bare room, then pinned her with an unrelenting gaze.

'You try hard—I'll have to say that much for you. Everything's spotless, but this is no place for you.'

Kathryn knew the furniture was old and mismatched, the carpet faded and thin in places. The rooms were tiny and the building itself was in a poor section of town, but it was her home and she wouldn't apologise for any of it. 'I'm sure it doesn't meet with your approval, but I wouldn't expect you to see the charm it holds for me. You have no place here, Logan. Nothing in it reminds me of you.'

'Did you find me so hard to forget?'

She bunched her fists at her sides and stood staring at that handsome face with the hint of a smile playing about his lips, hating him more than ever before. He knew! No matter how many times she had tried to put him out of her mind during the last five years, he never would stay forgotten. And even now, with arrogant sureness, he knew nothing had changed. Her voice was reduced to an angry whisper. 'Please, just leave me alone.'

He stepped closer to her. 'You left me once, Kathryn, but you'll never leave me again. I've spent years searching for you and now I've found you. You're mine!'

'You're wrong.'

'You loved me once. I knew it then, and it's still true now. I asked you to marry me and you said yes. Remember?'

She blinked rapidly at the dry sting of tears at the backs of her eyes. 'Stop it!'

Without thinking, Logan reached out to tangle

his fingers in her glorious hair. It was still thick and shining, tumbling its way far down her back, but she jerked away from him.

The small width of the room separated them as they both stood stiffly staring at one another like a hunter and his prey. The air crackled.

Kathryn struggled with herself. After all these years Logan was here, reminding her that she belonged only to him. His quiet strength unwillingly drew her to him, but she fought against the traitorous emotions she had long ago buried. 'How did you find me?' she choked.

'It wasn't easy. You led me one hell of a chase.'

'You didn't think I'd stay in Vancouver, did you? You underestimated me.' A fleeting white smile of acknowledgement passed his lips. 'All right, so you've found me. But it's all been a waste of time for you.'

He didn't say anything, just stood there smiling faintly.

The hair on the back of her neck stood on end and a knot of fear expanded in her chest, but she kept her face expressionless. She felt the calculating glitter of his eyes slashing from the top of her wind-tangled hair all the way to her feet, and shivered.

'I've come to take you home,' said Logan quite naturally, but all his muscles tensed as if he was about to spring.

'This is my home, Logan.'

He did spring then. His long fingers fastened on her shoulders, dragging her up close to him. 'Why? I wanted to give you everything! Everything I had was yours. But you walked away. You left me without a word, without a trace. Why?'

She trembled in his arms, looking up at him with tormented eyes, but before she could say a word, something snapped inside him, releasing his finger-hold of self-control. His big hands jerked to either side of her head, sliding through her hair, forcing her mouth up to his.

She knew she should resist him, but at the first touch of his hard demanding lips, the pain and disillusionment of the last five years rolled away as if it never existed. His tall broad body brushed against hers and her response was instinctive, wild with longing. His mouth burned against hers with demanding urgency. His fingers threaded through her glossy hair as she melted to all the hard angles and planes of his solid unyielding strength. He was warm and vibrant, and her arms unthinkingly circled his neck and shoulders.

She hadn't forgotten the texture of his body, the hardness of his rippling muscles, the smoothness of his skin, the thick springy blackness of his hair. He was her other half, the vital part that made her whole. When she had left him all those years ago she couldn't deny that her heart had stayed with him.

His kiss changed then, became gentle, lengthened and deepened, and she heard a low moan, but whether it came from her throat or his, she couldn't be sure. She was here in his arms again—Logan Ramsey, the man she loved, the man who had asked her to marry him.

But he had married her sister instead. She still had the newspaper clipping tucked away in a book somewhere. The picture of the happy couple and the accompanying article had covered half the society page. How could she forget even for a minute?

With an exclamation of self-disgust, her whole body clenched as she jerked herself out of his arms and crossed to the other side of the room on shaking legs. Her heart pounded in her throat and her breath came in short gasps, but she managed to keep her voice from wobbling. 'You'd better leave now. I don't think Carol would be too happy if she knew where you were or what you were doing.'

Logan let out a long shuddering breath and dragged his hands through his hair before pulling himself together. He threw her a sharp frowning glance full of a strange bitterness. 'Haven't you kept in contact with anyone? Any of your old friends? Do you expect me to believe you don't know?'

A wary look crossed her face at his ragged tone, and she unconsciously held a tiny breath. 'Know?'

'Your sister's dead! A heart ailment,' he said callously, not believing she didn't know. 'It was only a week after Jon was born.'

All her breath left her and she stared at him. She couldn't believe it. Looking at him standing across from her so tall and still, she managed to feel an unwanted sympathy cutting through her shock. 'I didn't know.' And then swiftly another thought struck her. 'Aunt Miriam must be frantic! You know how she always doted on her. Carol was her whole world—there wasn't anyone she loved more. I really should go to her. Maybe just being there might help. That's why you came, isn't it? Why didn't you say so at once?' Without waiting for his answer, she turned blindly towards her bedroom, intending to throw several things into an overnight bag, but Logan stopped her.

A strange expression flickered across his face, but he was quick to mask it. 'I'm glad you have sense enough to agree to come with me tonight, but there's really no great hurry. We'll go after you've had something to eat. No sense travelling on an empty stomach.'

She should have been warned by his lack of sorrow, his expressionless face, his whole attitude. But in Kathryn's frame of mind, she was only intent on helping her aunt through this terribly difficult time. Logan might not feel the loss as sharply as Aunt Miriam would. He had his lumber business to keep him occupied, but Aunt Miriam lived alone and had always centred her whole world on Carol. She would be devastated.

The meal Kathryn shared with Logan was quickly and tastefully prepared, but it could have been sawdust for all she cared. He washed up the dishes while she went to pack. It was understood that he would drive her as far as her aunt's home and like a blind fool, she leaned back and actually relaxed in the plush leather seat of his sports car as they drove to the northern outskirts of Vancouver.

If she began to remember how it used to be, sitting beside him like this, she put it out of her mind at once. It did no good to remember such things. That part of her life was over. Logan had proved to be a man of little substance. He was all fine talk and empty charm and still emptier promises. She had seen him for what he was, and she could only thank God her eyes had been opened before she had made the mistake of marrying him. It would have been a disaster. But all her barriers were once again in place, and they would stay there.

CHAPTER TWO

IT was only when they missed the turn-off to Aunt Miriam's house that Kathryn began to suspect something was wrong. She tensed and sat forward, peering out the windshield at the eerie shadows in the darkness on either side of the road. The traffic was thin at this time of night. They were leaving the city behind, driving into the wild and sometimes desolate timber country of British Columbia with its lush greenery dripping with rain. She felt nervous and uneasy, and she looked at Logan with rising suspicion.

'Where are you taking me?' she demanded tightly. 'You missed the turn-off.'

He easily negotiated a sharp bend in the road before flicking a cool glance at her. 'I'm taking you home, just as I intended.'

'But you said you'd take me to Aunt Miriam's!'

'No, I didn't. You assumed I would.'

'But——' she breathed harshly, 'she'll need somebody to be with her.'

'You didn't care about her for five years. Why the sudden concern now?'

Kathryn flushed. 'That's not true. It's not a sudden concern. She knows how much I care— I've kept in contact with her all these years.'

'But you never once came back to see her.'

I couldn't bear to be reminded, she wanted to tell him. Instead she said: 'No, I didn't come back, but we wrote to each other at least once a month.'

Logan's face was like finely chiselled granite. 'I know. I read all your letters.' He ignored her sharp indrawn breath and went on callously, 'You very conveniently omitted your return address, so there was never any way she could get in touch with you, was there? She wrote, but she could never post the letters. She could never tell you all the things she wanted you to know. For five years she got letters postmarked from all over the world. She had to read about how well you were doing—all the wonderful places you'd seen, the things you'd done, the people you'd met. But you never fooled her for one minute.'

Kathryn turned her face away and breathed deeply, trying to control her rapidly mounting shame at having been found out. 'I have a friend in a travel agency who arranged to mail the letters for me. I thought it best to do it that way so as not to worry her.'

Logan gripped the steering wheel so tightly his knuckles turned white. 'But she was worried. When Carol died, she was sick, she had no one to turn to. She kept hoping you'd read about it in the papers and come home. But you never came . . .'

Kathryn jerked her head up and felt her skin prickle as a sudden icy coldness swept over her. 'You make it sound——' She swallowed hard and clenched her hands in her lap before she said very softly: 'Carol didn't die recently, did she? She's been dead a long time. How long, Logan?'

He slowed the powerful car and turned

slightly towards her. 'A little more than four years ago.'

'*You tricked me!*' she cried. 'You made it sound like she died only yesterday. How could you?'

'You jumped to conclusions. I merely took advantage of the opportunity.'

She fumed in the explosive silence that fell between them, 'I should have known how low you'd stoop! What other things do you have up your sleeve for me?' She glared sarcastically. 'I suppose you'd be happy to spring it on me that Aunt Miriam's dead too? Knowing what a snake in the grass you are, nothing would surprise me!'

A harsh spasm of pain flashed across his face before he jerked his car to the side of the road and pulled to a stop, keeping the engine running. His hands curled into fists, striking the steering wheel over and over before curling around it with crushing power. His whole body was stiff and strangely rigid. 'You're right, Kathryn—you have lost your aunt too. But before she died, she made me promise to find you and take care of you.'

Her heart stopped like a frozen fist in the middle of her chest as the cruelty of his words rolled over her. She couldn't utter a sound.

'I'm sorry,' he muttered. 'I shouldn't have said it like that, but you——' He put his head in his hands and slumped forward, resting his elbows on the steering wheel. 'She was sick for a long time. Cancer, they said. She died last month.'

Everything was still, Kathryn's eyes closed, remembering the woman who had given her so much.

'It was never my intention to trick you,' he said

gently. For years I've had private investigators following up your letters, trying to find you. Not only for her—for me too. Several weeks ago one finally succeeded. I've followed you for days now and tonight I fully intended to tell you about her straight off. Only I couldn't find the words—especially since you didn't know about Carol either. But I did make it clear I intended to take you home with me.'

'Because you promised my aunt.' The whispered words were squeezed from her throat.

'Because it's where you belong.' He turned to her in the close confines of the car and took her ice-cold hands in his, looking deeply into her stricken blue eyes. 'You've lost your family, but you still have me. You'll always have me.'

She blinked and shuddered as the reality of his words punctured her shock. As she pulled her hands out of his crushing grip, her voice was quiet and coolly dignified. 'Thank you, Logan. You can consider your promise to a dying woman fulfilled. You found me. But I'm capable of taking care of myself and I prefer to be independent. Any obligation you might have felt is at an end.'

'No, it's not,' he said just as quietly, searching her white face in the gloom. 'You're coming home with me. You have me—and my son. We'll be married——'

Her eyes flew up to his. 'Yout can't mean that!'

'You promised to marry me five years ago. You'll keep that promise now!'

'Do you honestly expect me to go home with you? To the house my sister lived in? To assume her role as your wife? To care for her child as if I were his mother?' Kathryn's shrill voice rose with each question and bordered on hysteria.

He turned abruptly away from her, his eyes smouldering with angry impatience, and backed his car on to the road. 'You made me a promise, then vanished without keeping it. I've never found out why but you're going to tell me and we'll go on from there. I've searched for you all this time without giving up, thinking only of what might have been, what almost was. You still love me, Kathryn—I know you do. It's there in the way you move, the way you look, only you're afraid to admit it. You're mine. You'll never leave me again!'

They drove the rest of the way in silence, and it was only when they passed through a massive iron gateway dully glinting in the watery moonlight that Logan broke the strained silence between them.

'This was my parents' house,' he said in a roughly quiet voice. 'Carol never lived here. I don't know if she even knew about it.' The car continued to purr along a tree-lined drive with dim lights set low against the ground to guide the driver towards the house and the quiet hum of the engine made his grim voice that much more unsettling. 'I brought Jon here for the first time yesterday. Until now, I've simply considered this the big empty house where my brother and I grew up. Now, together, we can make it a happy home.'

His eyes clashed with hers in a silent challenge before she let out the breath she was unconsciously holding. 'You're taking entirely too much for granted. I'll admit I thought I was in love with you once, just as I thought you loved me. But that was a long time ago. We've both changed since then and you married my sister. That alone makes everything different now.'

'Your sister's dead,' Logan said in a harsh implacable voice, not taking his eyes off her as the car came to a stop outside the front door. 'I won't let her come between us—not now, not ever. Later we'll talk about her. This isn't the time or the place. We'll be married tomorrow— I've already got the licence.' He patted his pocket and a small smile hovered at the corners of his mouth. 'This is your home now. I've told the housekeeper we're already married, so when you see her, don't be surprised if she calls you Mrs Ramsey.'

Kathryn's jaw dropped. 'How—— You can't force me, Logan. I won't marry you!'

Grim determination settled in his eyes. 'Don't be too sure about that. When I want something, I never give up until it's mine. Surely you remember that much about me?'

'I won't be one of your possessions,' she said with a shiver, remembering when she had been his secretary how he was able to use his charm and keen wits whenever his money failed to bring the desired results in his lumber business. 'You'll never own me. I have a mind and a will of my own.'

His laugh was full of arrogant sureness when he walked around to the other side of his car, opening her door with an exaggerated bow. 'You know I'll wear you down in the end. All these years of searching for you have taught me infinite patience. Your mind and your will may be your own, but everything else about you belongs to me. You're mine, Kathryn!'

Since it was so late, no one greeted them when they entered the house. Only a small brass lamp burning on an elegant claw-footed table in the entrance hall gave any evidence that they were expected. Logan led her up a wide curving staircase thickly carpeted in a pale shade of muted green. On the light panelled walls, large gilt-framed portraits watched their silent progress. All along the hallway, she was conscious of small tables holding expensive sculpture in marble, bronze and wood. Here, too, were magnificent oil paintings, Italian masters, but Logan's firm silent strides on the thick carpet carried him past them all without a second glance. He stopped outside an ornate wooden door and waited for Kathryn to catch up to him before he pushed it open.

This bedroom was at the front of the house overlooking the front lawn with its circular drive. It was large and airy and the subtle pastel shades of ivory and gilt furniture made the room seem even larger than it was. A French Provincial four-poster bed covered with a delicate ivory satin spread was at one end with several gilt-edged chairs and intricately carved chests scattered comfortably about the rest of the room. There were sparkling crystal bottles on a dainty dressing table, and she knew they must contain expensive perfumes.

Without a word, Logan set her suitcase on the floor before his glittering gaze rested on her profile. Kathryn turned away nervously and picked up one of the crystal containers. Her nose wrinkled in surprise at the unmistakable scent of Shalimar, and she remembered him once telling her he preferred the lighter floral scent she used to wear when they were dating to the more heavy exotic ones other women favoured. She wondered whose room this was, but kept silent, not trusting herself to say anything.

'I want you to be happy here,' he said quietly enough, but his tone was cold and authoritative. 'The bathroom is through that door.' He pointed in the general direction to his right. 'Beyond it is my room. Have a bath, if you like—there's plenty of hot water. And try to rest. Tomorrow will be a busy day.'

He waited a moment as if he expected her to comment, but she still didn't trust herself to speak, and he turned away with a grim tightening of his lips, nodding briefly, and left her.

A pale Aubusson carpet silenced her footsteps when she walked to the long windows and pushed aside the filmy ivory draperies to look outside to the green perfection of the lawn dappled in rainy moonlight. A deep shudder passed over her and, resting her forehead against the cool gleaming glass, she bit back a sudden sob and tried to shake off a sudden nervousness.

What was she doing here? Logan had tricked her and now he thought she was trapped. Her head spun. Carol might have been able to make herself at home in such opulent surroundings, but this was no place for Kathryn. She could never be at home in a mansion filled with expensive furnishings that must have cost the earth. It belonged to Logan Ramsey, the wealthy lumber man who appreciated its worth and took it for granted.

There was a time when she thought her world and his could mesh, but she had been so very young and idealistic then. At nineteen she had thought love could overcome the obstacle of their different backgrounds, but that was before he had betrayed her and married her sister three months later. Her eyes were wide open now. She was just an ordinary person, unsophisticated but full of integrity. Something inside her refused to be forced to stay here with no say in the matter. She had her dignity to maintain, and her pride, which was no small thing.

She went over the things she knew about Logan. He was thirty-five years old, handsome, shrewd, intelligent, dangerously charming and very wealthy. But the blindness of love was removed now, and all those qualities didn't add up to someone she wanted to spend the rest of her life with. Somehow she would find a way to leave, and it wouldn't be a cowardly flight in the middle of the night like last time . . .

It was early when she woke the next morning. In spite of a restless tossing and turning, she managed to sleep for several hours, knowing she would need it if she was going to leave here on her own two feet. A slight tinkling sound disturbed her and she thought she heard a dog barking in the far distance. She was lying on her stomach with her face buried in her arms when she felt she was not alone in the room. She flicked open one eye before turning over and sitting up with a jerk.

A small, extremely thin boy dressed in well worn gym shoes, blue jeans, and a bright blue sweat shirt stood by the side of her bed, idly fingering the stopper of one of the crystal bottles that had been on the dressing table. He studied her intently with big solemn blue eyes that were exactly like Logan's. He didn't smile. For a long moment he just continued to stare at her. When he did speak, she was stunned by what he said.

'Are you my mom?' he asked quite seriously.

Kathryn drew her breath in sharply, but when she didn't answer him, he went on: 'My dad said he was going to find my mom and bring her back here to live with us. Are you her?'

'You're—Jon?' came the strangled whisper.

He nodded slowly, looking down at the perfume bottle in his tiny hands. 'My name's Jonathan, but everybody calls me Jon. This is pretty, isn't it? Is it yours?'

'It's very pretty, but I don't know who it belongs to. Your father didn't tell me.'

A slight movement at the doorway caught her eye and she turned to see Logan standing there with a quiet dignity. Formally dressed but looking very much at ease in a charcoal grey suit with a brilliant white shirt and much lighter grey satin tie, he walked in as if he had every right. 'It was your grandmother's, like everything else in here, Jon,' he said coolly, ruffling the boy's shining black hair. He took the bottle and set it back on the table. 'Your mother prefers perfume that makes us think of summer sunshine and wildflowers.'

Jon's head immediately swivelled back to Kathryn. 'Then you *are* my mother!' In an instant he scrambled on to the bed and flung himself into her arms. 'Oh, I'm so glad!' His bear hug nearly choked her before he loosened his grip and knelt beside her, keeping his arms around her neck. His eyes were flashing and his whole thin face altered with a brilliant smile spreading from ear to ear. 'My dad told me you were beautiful, but I was afraid he didn't really mean it. You are! Just as beautiful as he said!'

A hectic wild red blush filled Kathryn's face. He was such a charmer, so innocent, so trusting, so ready to accept whatever his father told him. But he was not her child; he was Carol's. She couldn't be his mother. Anger bubbled up in her throat, but she was forced to swallow it back. No matter what she said it would hurt him.

'Jon, will you go and tell Mrs Gresham your mother's awake and we'll be down to breakfast in just a few minutes?' Logan said quietly with an engaging smile. 'I want to say good morning to your mother and then I'll be right down.' He lifted his son off the bed and watched him race out of the door.

When they were alone, Kathryn threw him a furious look. A deep flush was still on her face and her bright blue eyes flashed with anger. 'You don't play fair! How could you say things like that to him?'

'All's fair——' he began to quote.

'—We know this isn't love,' she broke in bitterly, 'so it must be war.'

Logan flicked a smouldering look at her sitting in the bed in a spotless white nightgown with tiny wildflowers she had embroidered at the edge of the square neck and at the wrists of the long sleeves. Her long black hair was caught back and threaded with a narrow faded blue ribbon, making her look young and vulnerable. 'You aren't dressed for war,' he said softly, sitting on the edge of the bed beside her, 'but you are dressed for——'

'Don't!'

A ghost of a satisfied smile flickered in his eyes. He bent closer to her. 'Ah, my innocent love, you're still mine. I've often wondered if there'd been anyone. But seeing you here, blushing furiously in your chaste white nightgown while I sit so close, I have my answer. You're mine. You were always mine. And now Jon, because he's my son, has a claim on you too.'

'No!' she cried harshly. 'He's Carol's son. I can't be his mother. Carol was your wife—I won't take her place!'

There was a disquieting glitter in his eyes. 'Jon knows about Carol. Even though he's not yet five, he's old enough to know. I told him she died a week after he was born. I also told him about you.' He got to his feet and walked with jerky steps up and down the room, his hands shoved deep in his pockets. His face was inscrutable when he swung back to her. 'You're the only woman I ever wanted to be the mother of my children, Kathryn. You'll be my wife—the kind of wife Carol never was.'

'I don't believe I'm hearing this,' she said in desperation. 'How can you say such things now that she's dead and can't defend herself? Whatever we might have had is over. It has to be. Can't you see that? When it came right down to it, you chose her.'

'I didn't choose! She was—there.' He dragged his hands roughly through his hair. 'It's not over between us. It was never over. I've gone to a lot of trouble to find you and I won't let you leave me again.'

'Carol will always be between us.'

Logan turned abruptly and walked to the window, brooding at the thunder clouds forming low in the sky. 'Carol and I shared the Ramsey name and wealth. Nothing else mattered to her.'

Kathryn breathed in harshly. 'You shared a son.'

He didn't turn back to look at her for a long time, but when he finally did, his eyes were bleak. His face was a peculiar grey and she had the distinct impression he was struggling with himself. He started to say something, then stopped as if he couldn't really find the right words. He studied her face, then lifted his shoulders in a resigned shrug. 'I won't allow her to come between us, Kathryn. Jon needs you. He's the most important one right now. These are the formative years of his life. You've seen him. He's so solemn and quiet. He's a lot older than his years, and that's not good. He's never known what it's like to have a mother love him— and believe me, that can be a terrible thing.' His face twisted as if he was remembering something unpleasant but it quickly passed. 'You can change all that. He—likes you. It was an instinctive thing, it wasn't put on.'

She glared at him. 'You're using your son, Logan! Haven't you any scruples?'

His face was blank for a moment, then he began to smile. 'Drastic situations call for drastic measures. You love children. I watched you for days at the nursery school—I knew that was the only way I could reach you. Come on, admit it. You won't disappoint Jon. He's finally going to have the mother I've always wanted for him.' His eyes gleamed like quicksilver as he crossed the room and reached out to tuck a soft black curl behind her ear.

It was an intimate gesture that made the heat rush to her face and her heart pound in her ears. She slid off the bed and stood facing him from the opposite side of it. 'I'm his aunt. If you want me to care for him, all right, I'll do it. But don't ask me to step into Carol's shoes and be your wife.'

His indulgent smile turned into a scowl. 'That really sticks in your throat, doesn't it? Well, it sticks in mine too. I'd like to forget she ever existed, and from the things I've heard about how she ran you ragged with her demands when you both were growing up, I'd imagine you would too. Let's put her behind us. She's gone. Let her stay in the past.'

Kathryn lifted her chin and squared her shoulders. There was a cold dignity in the way she stood facing him. 'You really are heartless, aren't you? Carol had your son. That's something you can't change.'

'Oh, but I can.' Logan swiftly came around the bed, trapping her against the wall, gripping her shoulders, bringing her face close to his. 'You're Jon's mother now—because I say so. And you'll be my wife in a few hours—because a judge says so. He happens to be a friend of mine and we've pulled some strings to make it all legal. You—are—mine!'

'I can't be your wife. You can't ask that of me!' Too much had happened, and she could never forgive him.

He shook her and his voice was ragged. 'I'm not asking. That's already behind us. I asked you five years ago and you said yes. But you don't have to worry that I'll force myself on you. I've never yet taken an unwilling woman and I don't intend to start with you. I told you, one thing I've learned in my search for you is patience. You're going to come to me freely, when the time is right. That's the only way it can be. I know you still love me, even though you won't admit it to yourself yet, and I'm content to wait until you do.' He let her go then and walked to the door with firm unhurried strides. 'Wear something pretty today,' he added. 'This is a day all brides wish to remember, isn't it?'

It was a day Kathryn would much rather forget. She was being manipulated, and everything inside her rebelled. There had to be some way out of this mess. Logan might think he had everything under control, but she'd show him how wrong he was!

Half an hour later, Jon stood waiting for her at the bottom of the wide staircase and led her to the breakfast room, where he proudly introduced her to Mrs Gresham, their housekeeper.

'Here she is,' he said with a grin. 'My mom!'

Emma Gresham, a rosy round woman with silvery hair styled in soft waves, extended her hand and beamed at Kathryn. 'I'm so glad you're here, Mrs Ramsey. Jon's been a regular magpie this morning. I'm absolutely astounded by the change in him!'

Kathryn frowned slightly, shaking her hand before looking at Jon. He grinned up at her and pressed close to her side, slipping his tiny hand into hers without the least sign of selfconsciousness.

Mrs Gresham's watery eyes sparkled and her body shook with mirth. 'See what I mean? He was always so solemn and quiet before. Kept to himself, mostly. Never could get him to say more than two words at a time, most days. And he wouldn't let anyone touch him either. Now look at him! He's actually holding your hand and he hasn't stopped grinning this past half hour.' She ruffled Jon's hair and patted his bony shoulders in a goodnatured way and gave Kathryn another beaming smile of welcome, then started towards the kitchen. 'And that's the first time I ever remember him not flinching when I ruffled his hair. Breakfast is almost ready. Now I suppose Jon will have a good appetite too, to go along with all the other sudden changes,' she grinned. 'Make yourself at home, Mrs Ramsey. I'll be back in a minute.'

Kathryn seated herself at the massive round table and Jon pulled his heavy chair quite close to hers, looking up expectacntly. She gave him an uncertain smile, resenting the feeling that somehow she had just lost another battle. Logan was not alone any more. Now there were two of them tugging at her heart, and it wasn't fair! Abruptly, she turned away and her eyes travelled nervously around the room.

It was long and wide and shining, even with the boiling grey clouds closing in against the windows. Someone had placed a small bowl of wildflowers in the centre of the table and the delicate colour of their petals was a stark contrast to the heavy ivory damask tablecloth and glittering crystal and silver there. The walls were panelled in limed oak and bright gold curtains with heavy valances glinted at the long windows, matching the thick golden-toned Oriental carpet on the floor. It could have been a cheerful room, but the ponderous furniture was crowded and oppressive. The table was too big, the chairs too heavy. It was almost as if whoever had decorated this room was determined to flaunt the fact that money was no object. Only the flowers were out of place. And then she realised they were made of silk and Jon was looking at her mischievously.

'I brought them in from the other room because they're pretty and they're like the ones on your nightgown.'

Kathryn's throat closed up and she felt a dangerous tug at her heartstrings. 'Thank you, Jon. That was really very thoughtful of you.' Her voice wobbled and she began to blink rapidly. 'This is a big house, isn't it?' she rushed to change the subject. 'Er—how do you manage to remember your way around?'

'It's awfully big, isn't it?'

She laughed helplessly. 'I'm afraid I'd get lost without a map!'

His little face was suddenly serious. 'If you ever do get lost, I'll find you.' And then after a small stretching silence he said: 'My dad told me it took him five years to find you. You won't ever go away again, will you?'

She caught her breath sharply and lifted her chin. Thin shards of ice shuddered down her spine and then she spotted Logan standing in the doorway watching her, as intent on her answer as Jon was. Her eyes clashed with his for a screaming moment. Damn him! How could he put his son up to this?

'Your dad told you that?' she breathed, still looking at Logan.

Jon nodded and kept his solemn eyes on her face as it rapidly lost all its colour. 'He said your sister died, but he was going to find you and bring you back to see me some day. He said—he said——' He swallowed hard and struggled to his feet, shaking all over.

Helplessly, Kathryn put her arms right around him, holding him tightly against her, absorbing his shudders until his rigid little body began to relax.

He muttered into her shoulder, 'He said you were the one who should have been my mother and when you came back and talked to me, you'd never leave again. You won't, will you?'

The silence was thick and heavy as she

continued to hold him, then she looked down into his eyes and felt a slight shock run through her, almost a recognition. Being Carol's, he had her own blood in his veins. This was the closest she would ever have to a son of her own. 'No, Jon,' she finally whispered, her chin lifting a fraction, her breath stirring the black silk of his hair. 'No, I won't ever leave you. Your dad was right. Once I saw you and spoke to you, how could I leave?'

She didn't trust herself to look at Logan again. She knew his face would be full of triumph. But she would never admit defeat. He might have won this battle, but the war was just beginning.

CHAPTER THREE

AT one o'clock that afternoon the storm that had
threatened all morning finally broke. They drove
through heavy winds and through a strange grey
darkness split by bright flashes of lightning and
dull rolling thunder. The rain fell in big
spattering drops, pounding mercilessly on their
shoulders as they ran up the steps to the
courthouse. Logan tried to keep Kathryn from
getting drenched, but an umbrella was useless in
the wind, and once inside the building, he turned
to look at her and saw that she was soaked.

'Not a very auspicious beginning for us, is it?'
he said quietly, regretfully, before taking her coat
and shaking it on the tiled floor.

Kathryn stood still and silent, not trusting
herself to say anything. The length of her black
hair glittered with bright sparkling drops of
water. The dress she wore, one of her better
efforts at dressmaking, was a bright blue wool the
colour of a summer sky, and it heightened the
ivory pallor of her skin.

Logan took off his own coat with a grim
tightening of his lips and together they went in
search of the judge who was to perform the
ceremony.

Kathryn noticed no one was about as they
made their way down the dim quiet corridor and
somehow she was glad of it. She didn't want to

be offered any good wishes or congratulations. This was a sham of a marriage only for his son's benefit, and she couldn't bear the thought of pretending to be a happy bride.

Judge Hammond was a big, balding, affable man who greeted them with a wide smile. 'Come in, come in,' he said. 'I've been waiting for you.' He gripped Logan's hand with genuine friendliness, then turned to Kathryn with a delving look that made her squirm. 'And Kathryn Marshall. Well, well! Logan's told me a lot about you.'

She looked back at him steadily but didn't smile in return.

A vague frown crossed his face as he gestured for them to be seated in the two cracked leather chairs in front of his littered desk. 'Now then,' he cleared his throat noisily, 'I have to ask you a few questions, Miss Marshall. Er—to make sure this marriage is legal. You understand?'

She nodded faintly, wondering what he would do if he knew the real reason for this marriage. Would he be shocked? Perhaps not, she decided. At his age and in his position, he probably wouldn't be surprised at anything.

'Are you a willing party to this marriage?' he asked quietly.

She continued to look at him without wavering and her voice was clear and cold. 'Yes, I am.'

'You're not being coerced in any way?'

Kathryn felt rather than saw Logan stiffen beside her. His hands were resting lightly on the arms of his chair, but she could feel his rigid body vibrating. She turned and met his unflinching eyes but couldn't read any expression in them. And then she thought she saw them flicker with a fleeting regret, and it startled her.

'No, sir,' she said after a long minute, still looking at Logan, 'I'm not being coerced. I want to marry Logan.'

The judge leaned forward, his hands folded on top of the untidy piles of paper littering his desk, peering at her from under bushy white eyebrows. 'Do you love this man?' he whispered.

A brilliant red blush ran up her neck and disappeared into her hair, and she quickly dropped her eyes to her lap where she twisted her hands together.

'Forgive me, my dear,' he said with a wide satisfied grin. 'I'm just a meddling old fool. Love is not a prerequisite for marriage, although it helps. I've known the Ramsey family for years and Logan, here, is like a son to me. I want him to be happy, that's all. You don't have to answer that question.'

He stood then and asked them to stand together so they could make their vows.

The ceremony was brief, and Kathryn moved like an automaton, speaking in a hoarse whisper when Logan's hand at her waist prodded her to say the proper words. His own voice was low and clear and firm, his hands steady when he slipped a thick shining gold wedding band on her finger. She nearly dropped the broad masculine circle of gold that was his. Her hands shook so much when she tried to slide over his knuckle that in the end he had to put it on himself. There was no perfunctory kiss, although she was sure the judge expected one, and she couldn't quite conceal her relief when Logan stepped away from her.

It was only after she had signed her name to a legal-looking document that she noticed the others in the room. They were two nondescript little men who hurriedly signed their names under hers and Logan's before bowing deeply and leaving as silently as they had come.

Witnesses, she thought. All legal and above board. He hadn't forgotten anything. And suddenly anger stiffened her backbone. His marriage to Carol hadn't been any hole-and-corner thing. Their ceremony had been held in a church. Carol had worn a beautiful white lace gown and carried orchids. Hundreds of people had met them as they stepped into the brilliant sunshine, flashbulbs exploded and rice was showered, and their pictures were plastered in every newspaper across the country.

But here she was in a dingy little office that reeked of disinfectant, before a judge who was an old friend of Logan's family, with two unknown witnesses who were probably paid handsomely to keep their mouths shut. What a difference! But then her whole life with Logan would be entirely different from what he had shared with Carol. For one thing, there would never be any more children for him. She swallowed hard and managed to force a small smile to her colourless face.

Judge Hammond had gone back to his desk and was pouring a dark yellow liquid into three small glasses on a tray. 'May you have a long and happy marriage,' he said loudly, holding up his glass to theirs. 'And may I soon be called on to be the godfather of your first child together.' He slapped Logan soundly on the back and grinned goodnaturedly at Kathryn's hectic blush as she only pretended to sip the drink.

They didn't go back home when they left the judge's chambers. Logan took her to an elegant little restaurant where he was obviously well known. The maître d' greeted them with an expansive smile and led them to a secluded table for two near wide windows covered with burnished gold curtains.

When Logan asked that they be opened, the man looked surprised, but quickly did as he was asked. 'Terrible day to be out, Mr Ramsey,' he murmured, looking at the wild rainswept scene before them.

'It's all in how you look at it, Antoine.' Logan gave him a wide boyish grin. 'Today is the most wonderful day for me!'

An expression of utter surprise crossed the man's face. 'You're the only one who has said so all day!' Then he laughed and called the waiter to bring the wine list to this honoured guest.

'What shall it be, darling?' Logan asked wryly before the waiter came. 'Champagne and caviar to celebrate?'

All the colour left her face and she stared at him with sick shock. 'You wouldn't!'

'Why not? The last time I tasted champagne was the day you promised to marry me. Remember?' His eyes narrowed. 'Five years, Kathryn. It's only fitting we should share it today. You're my wife now, not my fiancée. It's been a long time coming.'

'Please don't,' she whispered.

'Why? Don't you want to be reminded of that day? I remember it in great detail. You sat across from me in an elegant French restaurant, smiling, radiant with happiness. Your eyes had stars in them, big shining blue ones. You'd never tasted champagne or caviar before, you told me. It was a day of firsts for you.'

Kathryn squeezed her eyes tightly shut. It was a day of firsts, all right. Logan was sitting across from her now, looking so handsome in his suit and tie, but a more forceful picture of him danced in her memory. Time and time again she tried to erase it, but it was always there and it always came, unbidden, when she least expected it.

She could see his powerful muscular body gleaming in the sultry moonlight under the pines near Aunt Miriam's house. His naked skin had a silvery, unreal translucence. And then she saw Carol, naked too, her face close to his as they locked together in a passionate embrace, consumed by a roaring fire of their own making, oblivious to everyone and everything else except the sensuous pagan pleasure they found in each other.

What was it Logan had said to her only hours before? 'Kathryn, be my wife. Let me love you the way you were meant to be loved.'

A black and bitter rage welled up in her throat, but she shivered and tried to pull herself together, concentrating on the lightning splitting the boiling sky with broken spears of splintered silver. 'I haven't forgotten that day,' she whispered. 'And you're right, it was a day of firsts for me.' She had never before experienced betrayal.

The waiter came and went and she hadn't realised he had taken Logan's order until he set a small plate in front of them. She looked at the dark mound and nearly gagged. 'You're the one who's forgotten, Logan. I didn't like it. Too salty, remember?' Then her face hardened and she became calm, controlling the impulse to throw the caviar in his face. 'You really should be more careful not to confuse me with Carol.'

He laughed shortly, watching the faint colour stealing back into her face. 'Don't worry, I'll never do that. For one thing, Carol was a lot like my mother. She had expensive tastes, too. It didn't matter what it was as long as it cost a lot of money—and as long as everyone knew how much she paid for it. But not you, my love, never you.'

'Your money never meant anything to me,' Kathryn whispered vehemently.

'I know it.' His expression hardened and his eyes narrowed. 'I never could find your price. You're the only woman I couldn't buy, yet you could have had it all. I wanted to give you everything I had, but you walked away from me. Why, Kathryn? Tell me now. For five years I've wanted to know. Why did you leave me?'

The muted sounds in the room suddenly sounded loud in the silence between them, the murmur of voices, the chink of silver, the dull thud of a plate being set on a table. Somewhere near, ice tinkled in a crystal goblet as waiters passed by on soft cat-like feet. And over it all, heavy rain lashed against the windows and thunder rolled dimly in the distance.

She returned his intent stare without flinching, her voice as cold and calm as the icy quality of his eyes. 'I finally saw for myself that you were no different from any other man. All the illusions were gone. I'd have been a fool to trust you with my love.'

Logan stared at her incredulously, then his mouth twisted as several conflicting emotions ran across his face. 'You left me because I didn't live up to some ideal you'd set up in your mind?' He couldn't believe it. 'I never pretended to be anything other than what I am—an ordinary man.' He looked almost bewildered. 'Who opened your eyes, my innocent?'

'You did,' she said bitterly. 'You—and Carol. Now tell me something. Why did you marry her? And so soon after I left?'

A dull red filled his face, but his expression became hard and fixed. 'She needed my name.'

Kathryn was suddenly still, her face whitened and then her hand clenched on the table. The room rocked all around her. She supposed she should have been thankful he hadn't denied it but his bluntness stunned her. 'She was pregnant,' she said in a dull voice, 'and you had to marry her.'

'She *told* you?'

'No. But I should have known, shouldn't I? Carol was that kind of girl. It was bound to catch up with her sooner or later.' A helpless bitter laugh escaped her. *But why did it have to be you?* she wanted to scream at him. *You knew how much*

I loved you. She closed her eyes on a spasm of pain and saw again that haunting picture, their bodies cleaving together in the silvery moonlight . . .

'You disappoint me,' said Logan with a curious kind of anger in his face. 'I knew you were a romantic, full of girlish dreams, but I never thought you were a fool. You set up some impossible ideal in your head and then left me because I couldn't live up to it. Don't you know anything about men? There's not a one of us who's perfect.' His voice became hoarse and he clenched a fist and struggled with himself. The lines about his mouth were etched with pain. 'All that wasted time . . . If it's any consolation to you, you aren't the only one disillusioned. I thought we had something special. I thought our love was such that we could talk to each other about anything. Instead, you took the easy way out and ran away.'

Kathryn stared at him, quivering with anger. How dared he turn things around and make it look as if she was at fault? She did what anyone with an ounce of self-respect would have done. She didn't know much about men, but he didn't have to take what Carol offered, did he? He could have resisted that particular urge, couldn't he? 'It wasn't the easy way, Logan,' was all she could manage.

'Well, we've both got our eyes wide open now and perhaps it's for the best. We'll simply put the past behind us and go on from here. I want you to remember one thing, though. You became my wife today, but more importantly, you became

Jon's mother. Try to remember that, will you?'
He flicked back his cuff and glanced at the slim
gold watch on his wrist. 'When we're through
here, we'll go to my office. Dennis McIntyre's
drawn up some papers for you to sign—making
sure you're named Jon's guardian if anything
should happen to me.'

She watched him down a full glass of
champagne in one gulp and sensed his complete
withdrawal from her. He continued to sit there
looking at her, but she knew all he was seeing was
a little boy's solemn face. He was the important
one. There was nothing else left between them.

The rain continued to pummel them with
blinding wet fists as they entered his office
building, and Kathryn gave up trying to keep
dry. Her hair was plastered against her face in
spiky black tendrils and her coat was soaked.
When she walked, she made a pecular squishing
sound.

Logan towered beside her in the elevator,
totally unaffected by the elements. His coat and
shoes had shed the water. Only his hair shone
blue-black with bright crystal drops. He stood
tall and proud and silent, allowing nothing, not
even the weather, to touch him.

Everything was still when they stepped into the
corridor. The rain couldn't be heard here. When
he opened the door to his office, a slender blonde
woman seated behind her desk greeted him with
an expectant smile.

'Logan—Mr Ramsey—I've missed you!'

'Hello, Margaret,' he said with an absent nod.

'You make it sound as if I've been gone a long time.'

'You haven't been here for almost a week—that's a long time for you.' Cool and poised, she laughed up at him with an open invitation in her eyes before turning her attention to Kathryn. 'Are you together?'

He picked up a stack of letters from the desk, idly flipping through them, and before Kathryn could say anything he said: 'Dennis McIntyre's supposed to meet us here at three. When he comes, show him in, will you?' He started towards his office and said very quietly: 'And yes, Kathryn and I are together, Margaret. You can be the first to congratulate us. We were married today.'

Margaret stiffened, her face lost all its colour and she blinked at him with dazed brown eyes. Then all at once she pulled herself together and gave him a breezy smile that didn't fool Kathryn for a minute. 'Why, congratulations! I—I hope you'll be very happy.'

Logan nodded and disappeared into his office, but Kathryn just stood there looking at her with compassion. It was obvious Margaret was in love with him. She probably had hoped against hope he would notice her as something more than just the girl who efficiently ran his office. She had been in that position herself once, and when Logan began paying attention to her, she had bloomed like a rose starving for sunshine.

'I'm sorry he broke it to you like that,' she said softly.

Margaret turned quickly to a file cabinet and fumbled with the drawer before opening it.

Kathryn saw her shoulders quiver and knew her poise was slipping badly. 'Believe me, if I had known——'

'Stop it, Mrs Ramsey!' she whispered with venom. 'I don't want your pity. There isn't any need for it.'

Kathryn took an involuntary step backward in surprise and flinched at the malevolence in Margaret's flashing brown eyes.

'He's not the only Ramsey man. I'll just have to change my tactics and concentrate on Paul. His divorce should be final by now.'

Kathryn put a dazed hand to her face. 'Paul?'

'Logan's brother—his other half. Paul Ramsey, the concert pianist,' Margaret spat. 'Almost as handsome, almost as rich. Not half the man Logan is, but his money should make up for it.' She shrugged her slim shoulders and turning, smoothed her hands down the sides of her beige and brown silk suit, once again in control.

Kathryn could only stand and gape at her.

Could she really switch so easily from one brother to the other? Or was that simply hurt pride talking? She'd never met Paul, but she remembered his voice on the telephone when she used to work here. It was like rich dark velvet. Her romantic heart used to flutter when she thought of him giving concerts in all those European cities before kings and queens and great statesmen. She had hoped some day to meet this famous man, but she had never got around to it. Now he was her brother-in-law.

'Kathryn!' Logan's command finally penetrated her thoughts and her face filled with colour.

'Come in here, will you? I'm sure Margaret has more to do than stand around gossiping with you.'

Margaret's eyes narrowed, but Kathryn was too embarrassed to notice. She pulled herself together and followed him in silence.

Logan had removed his coat and rolled up his shirt sleeves and now he was looking out of the windows with a black scowl on his face. 'Take off your coat,' he said coldly, 'before you catch pneumonia.'

She didn't trust herself to answer him but did as he asked, then sat down quite still in one of the chairs in front of his desk.

Long minutes passed before he turned to look at her, and when he did, his eyes filled with cold blue flame. Her dress had dark wet patches across her shoulders and along the bodice where the rain had soaked through and her hair hung in heavy black ropes down her back. She could imagine the sight she made, especially if he compared her to his secretary with her impeccable silk suit and shining cap of blonde hair. His face was grim for a moment, then without a word he wrenched open the door to Margaret's office and disappeared.

A sigh escaped her and suddenly everything began to spin. She closed her eyes for a moment to block out the never-ending rain whipping against the huge windows in front of her. What was she doing here anyway? If only this pressure would lift from her heart. If only she could erase the past five years and start all over again. If only she hadn't seen Logan and Carol. If only ... If only ...

'Kate? Kate?'

Someone was crushing her hand and then she felt an arm behind her shoulders and a cold glass against her lips.

'Are you all right, Kate?'

The voice was unfamiliar. And who was calling her Kate? No one ever called her that any more. Cold water trickled across her lips and down her chin before she blinked in confusion.

A tall thin brown-eyed man wearing glasses was peering at her intently. His thick moustache twitched so violently she wanted to laugh.

'Are you all right, Kate?' he asked.

She found that she was held close to Logan's broad chest. His arm was around her shoulders as he held a glass of water against her mouth. 'Drink this,' he said gently. It felt so good to be here she didn't want to move, but Logan's attorney, Dennis McIntyre, was standing in front of her looking about to panic.

'Dennis!' she whispered. 'You look so different with that awful moustache.'

He drew back abruptly, then let out a loud whoop of relieved laughter. 'Still the same old Kate! You gave us quite a scare.'

She felt Logan stiffen before he straightened and set her firmly in the chair and went back to his desk.

'What happened?' she asked with a shiver, missing the comforting warmth of his body.

'You fainted.' Logan's face was set in rigid lines as he flung himself angrily in his chair.

'Oh.' She felt very small.

'Don't let it upset you. Knowing Logan, he probably rushed you from one place to another without giving you a minute to catch your breath.' Dennis flashed her a grin. 'It's no wonder you fainted—marrying him on a day like this! If it's any indication of the way your life together will be——'

'—Never mind,' Logan broke with a scowl. 'Just get those papers for her to sign.'

'Now look, you might push me around on the tennis court, but here,' Dennis tapped the legal documents in front of him with a bony forefinger, 'I'm the boss. She's not going to sign these unless she's in full possession of her faculties. They wouldn't be enforceable otherwise.'

'Stop talking like a lawyer,' said Logan with an irritated sigh. 'I just want this finished so I can take her home. She's not the most robust person at the moment. I should think you'd see that for yourself, you're so busy ogling my wife.'

'I'm not ogling your wife! Kate was a friend of mine long before she ever met you.'

'You're both talking as if I'm not even here,' Kathryn said quietly, standing on rubbery legs, trying to stop the argument between them.

Logan frowned impatiently. 'You weren't, for a good five minutes.'

She flushed. 'I'm fine now. Where do you want me to sign?'

'I don't advise you to sign anything without reading it first,' Dennis said firmly.

Logan scowled at him. 'She knows I wouldn't ask her to sign anything unless it was in her best interests.'

'You're making her an independently wealthy woman as well as Jon's mother. She might as well be aware of it!'

The blood swiftly drained from her face and she stared at Logan with enormous stricken eyes. 'What's he saying?' she demanded.

Logan ran a hand through his hair and rubbed the back of his neck before swivelling his chair away from her to stare out of the window at the rain-lashed darkness. 'Just sign the papers,' he said, his lips thinning.

'No! You know I don't want your money!'

'You're my wife now. The money's yours whether you sign or not.'

'I'm not for sale!' She flung the words at him before pushing past Dennis and accidentally scattering his papers all over the floor. She didn't turn back but ran headlong out of the office.

Logan started to go after her, but Dennis stopped him. 'Let her go. Give her a few minutes to pull herself together. We'll send Margaret to the ladies' room for her when she's had time to realise what you're really trying to do.'

'Thanks a lot, big mouth,' Logan said harshly, watching the lawyer on his knees, red-faced, gathering up the papers. 'If you'd kept your mouth shut she'd have signed and we'd be on our way home. Now I've got to try to make her see reason, and somehow I don't think she'll do that. God! You saw her face. She really hates me!'

'Don't you think she has that right?' Dennis stood up and straightened the papers into a neat pile. 'You've made her your wife—anyone would think you'd try to understand her. But no, the mighty Logan Ramsey has to blunder his way in and use brute force, thinking only of himself, ordering her to sign these without explaining what they're all about. Kate's a person who responds to tact and gentle persuasion.'

'And just how do you know so much about my wife?' Logan's voice was menacing.

'I dated her when she was nineteen—just before she started working for you. That's the one big regret of my life: I never should have let her get away from me.'

'Then why did you? Or did she stop seeing you?'

Dennis smiled stiffly. 'One night I dropped in to see her without ringing first to make sure she was home. Carol answered the door. Need I say more?'

Logan's whole face congested with rage. 'You preferred Carol to Kathryn?'

'I wasn't the only one. You married Carol.'

'And you know why.'

'Yes, I know why.' Dennis shook his head sadly. 'But does Kate?'

'She knows I had to marry Carol because she was pregnant, but we didn't discuss it in detail. She didn't look ready to listen to reason. I don't know if I can make her understand.'

'You'd better try. You've married her, but she isn't yours yet. She may never be yours.'

'Margaret!' Logan bellowed for his secretary. 'Go to the ladies' room and bring Kathryn back here. Now!'

But when Kathryn had run out of the office she hadn't gone to the ladies' room. Instead, she had made a mad dash for the elevator and then out into the rainswept darkness, intent only on putting as much distance between herself and Logan as possible.

He thought he could buy her! Her face streamed with stinging raindrops and within a minute she was drenched from head to foot. But she felt nothing. She was conscious only of a burning humiliation. He had tricked her into marriage, playing on her sympathy, asking her to be a mother to his son. She had done it out of a sense of obligation to her sister's child, a tiny innocent victim of Logan's irresponsibility. But in attempting to pay her for it, he had robbed her of her self-respect, and that she could not tolerate. She would be a mother to his son, but she would not be bought.

CHAPTER FOUR

KATHRYN had no particular destination in mind when she ran through the streets in the cold wind-lashed rain. Lightning continued to stun her with brilliant blinding flashes of light followed by sudden blackness before booming thunder clapped loudly in her ears. Every once in a while she pushed a hand across her eyes, trying to sweep away the water flooding her face, but it was useless. The rain was so heavy she couldn't see where she was going. And then she had to laugh. What did it matter? There was nowhere to go.

When she stopped at a street corner trying to get her bearings, a strong gust of wind whipped around a tall building and struck at her, making her stagger backwards and nearly lose her footing.

'Miss? Oh, miss?'

She heard a voice and peered through the rain at a taxi standing by the kerb with the door open invitingly.

'You look like you could use a lift, miss,' the driver shouted above the wind.

Kathryn blinked, shivering, then spread her hands in a futile gesture. When she had run from Logan her handbag and coat were left behind. 'I—I haven't any money to pay you,' she explained.

'I'm just on my way home. It'll be my good deed for the day. Hop in, miss. You're not dressed for this weather.'

She was in no position to argue. 'Thank you,' she said shakily, getting into the car and slamming the door to close out the rain.

'That's all right, miss. You shouldn't be out on a day like this. Where to?'

She looked at the man's friendly face creased with compassion. He reminded her of Aunt Miriam. Without thinking, she gave him the address.

When the taxi drew up in front of the dilapidated house, the driver gave her a speculative frown. 'You sure this is the right place?'

It was dark and unwelcoming, abandoned looking. Weeds were thick and untended even now.

Kathryn turned to him and tried to keep her teeth from chattering. 'My aunt's been sick. It doesn't look quite so—so neglected inside.'

He threw her a wide smile full of relief. 'You be sure to get out of them wet clothes right away, miss. And fix yourself a nice hot cup of broth so's you don't get a chill. I got a daughter about your age myself and I sure wouldn't like it if she didn't take care of herself. You do that now, you hear?'

'Thank you,' she said with a grateful murmur. 'I will.'

Her dress was plastered to her slight figure when she pushed open the door and stepped into the driving rain. The rusting iron gate creaked on broken hinges as she picked her way through slippery weeds covering the walk. Thorns from an old overgrown rosebush tore at her legs and she stumbled in the darkness, blinking away the raindrops that mingled with the surprising tears that began to stream down her face. She didn't hear the taxi as it drove away with splashing tyres in the flooded street.

She breathed ragged gasps of air, as she dragged herself up the steps, pushing open the front door with an echoing crash that bounced off the walls of the tiny house. Stepping inside the dark hall, she peered through a green gloom. Everything was quiet in the musty dankness. All she could hear was the thick pounding of her heart drumming in her ears and the rapid chattering of her teeth.

'Aunt Miriam?' she whispered.

A streak of lightning ripped through the sky, brightening the interior of the small room, only to be followed by instant darkness and an ear shattering clap of thunder. She held her hands over her ears and crept from room to room in the intermittent light and darkness. Just for an instant the tiny living room was lit up and she could see the old empty rocking chair in the corner by the fireplace.

'Where are you, Aunt Miriam?' she cried in desperation. 'I'm home!'

Peals of thunder crashed about her and rumbled in the distance. The increasing pounding of the rain matched the throbbing pulse at her temples as she dragged trembling fingers through the wet blackness of her hair. Her soaked dress moulded itself to her like a second skin and icy gooseflesh prickled along her spine. Then a curious calm settled over her as she reached for the doorknob to the bedroom. Silently, she opened the door and went into the small cosy room. Her eyes became accustomed to the darkness and she could see clearly now. Everything was here just the way it had always been.

Moving slowly, almost as if mesmerised, she neared the old-fashioned feather bed that had been her aunt's pride and joy. Comfort and protection seemed to reach out and beckon her. Only here, in this house, had she known any tenderness and consideration. Long-forgotten childhood memories rushed in on her.

When the authorities had notified her and Carol that their parents had been involved in a fatal car crash, Aunt Miriam had been with them to comfort them. She had brought them here and settled them in this wide soft bed and told them they would never be shuffled in and out of foster-homes. They were a family, and she would see to it they would always be together.

Kathryn shivered as reaction set in. Taking off her soaked clothing, she sank down into the musty blankets. They were soft and warm, and she began to weep with a sudden shuddering release. Aunt Miriam was gone, and Carol. There was no one to turn to. She had never felt more totally abandoned or alone.

Time passed slowly, and as the storm outside began to abate, so did her own storm of weeping. Her eyes were swollen and parched as she lay in the silent darkness wishing for a blind oblivion to finally swallow her into forgetfulness. If only she hadn't seen Logan with Carol that night! How different things might have been. He was everything she had ever dreamed of: strong and proud and handsome. He was a man people looked up to instinctively. But then he betrayed her. Now there was Jon to consider. Jon— Logan's and Carol's son.

A cold damp numbness was seeping into her bones. She huddled into a tight ball of misery and humiliation, blocking out the past and not looking to the future. There was only now, and it was unbearable. She could feel herself sinking, down, down into a warm dark pit, and all at once she felt safe and secure and oddly at peace as her numbed body turned to that unrecognised warmth and embraced it. If only this oblivion could last for ever, she remembered thinking, and then she knew no more . . .

When she woke the next morning a brilliant streak of sunlight was streaming over her face. She had slept deeply, dreamlessly, and for the first time in years had been unusually comforted. She turned her head, starting to rise, blinking at the blinding light, but her hair caught on something. She tugged lightly, wondering what was holding her, then turned back to stare into the strong calm face of her husband.

He was lying beside her but on top of the blanket, wearing only the dark trousers he had worn yesterday, propped up on one elbow watching her, the long fingers of his other hand firmly tangled in her hair. 'Hello, my wife,' he said softly.

All Kathryn's breath left her in a rush and she swallowed wildly. Was she dreaming?

'I knew you'd look this beautiful first thing in the morning.' His voice was unsteady.

Her eyes swiftly darted away from the smouldering look in his eyes, but when they fell to the smooth skin of his chest, she felt a sudden strangling constriction in her throat and started to get up in sudden panic. But she swiftly fell back beneath the blankets. She had nothing on.

A smile crossed Logan's face as his hand left her hair and lightly traced the frantic pulse at the side of her neck. 'I love you, my beautiful wife,' he said gently.

She was completely stunned; her face burned, and it took a full minute for her to find her voice. 'Have you been here—all night—with—with me?'

'Most of it. After all, it was our wedding night, wasn't it?'

'How did you find me?'

'Where else could you go? I knew you'd come here eventually.' He felt her tremble. 'It's all right,' he murmured gently, 'I understand why you had to come. I was wrong not to bring you here myself.'

Kathryn's throat tightened with inexplicable tears, but she couldn't say a word.

Logan inched closer and his dark head bent helplessly to hers. His lips tantalised the sensitive skin at her neck as he shifted his weight and curved the heavy warmth of his body around the cool slenderness of hers. 'I used to dream of this,' he said unsteadily, the brush of his lips making her quiver.

Her heart thumped madly. She had dreamed it too—for years and years. And now he was here and it was no longer a dream. Her mouth instinctively reached for his, hesitantly at first, tentatively searching, as if she was about to wake up and find herself alone again. But she was not alone. Her arms came up around his neck, her trembling fingers threading through the thick black silk of his hair before curling into clinging fists. A sudden overwhelming urgency shot through her at his answering passion when he kissed her with a hunger that made her gasp.

Trembling, his hands probed beneath the blanket to find the warm shuddering contours of her slight body, his fingertips lightly running over her, caressing her skin, cupping the small swell of her breasts. He murmured almost incoherently: 'Oh, Kathryn—*Kathryn!* Let me love you the way you were meant to be loved.'

As bemused as she was, the words washed over her, and almost at once where he touched her, her skin began to crawl. He had said that once before—and then beatrayed her. The image of him with Carol rose up before her. This same powerful body had been entwined with Carol's, this same swarthy skin—only then it was silvery, translucent, almost unreal. But this was reality, and it came rushing at her with a sickening jolt.

Logan felt her stiffening withdrawal and levered himself up on his elbows, looking at her with glazed eyes, his quivering body still covering hers. 'Kathryn?'

A ragged choking sensation caught at her throat and dry tears stung her eyes. 'Oh God! Leave me alone!'

'Why?' he asked desperately. '*Why?* You know you want this as much as I do! You're my wife!'

'Carol was your wife. You only married me to care for your son!'

'Carol!' The name was a strangled sound as defeat swept through him and it was a full second before he rolled away from her, drained. Sighing heavily, he sat on the edge of the bed, flexing his muscled shoulders wearily. 'Why did you have to bring her between us?'

'She'll always be between us. Be honest enough to admit it.' Kathryn hunched her shoulders, turning away.

But at once his fingers dug into her soft flesh, pushing her flat on her back, making her look at him. 'Don't push me, Kathryn. This isn't the time or the place for explanations. We'll go home and clear up our misunderstandings.'

She squeezed her eyes shut on a wave of despair. This was no misunderstanding. She had *seen* him. And besides, even if there could be some doubt about what she had seen, there was still Jon. Carol had been pregnant with him before Logan married her.

A low sound of disgust rumbled in his throat as he turned away and reached for his shirt draped over the back of a chair and put it on before bending down for her dress lying in a puddle on the floor. It was still wet, a blue crumpled mass in his hands. 'You can't wear this—it's ruined.' He crossed to the other side of the room and came back with a silvery blue raincoat lined with silk and held it out to her.

'Whose is it?' she asked with wide eyes.

'Yours. I had it delivered to my office yesterday when I saw your old one wasn't waterproof.'

'I don't want it.'

His eyes darkened impatiently. 'Stop being such a fool!'

'I can't accept it.'

'If you don't want to wear it then go naked,' he said callously. 'Everything you had was ruined after yesterday's rain. You'll need a whole new wardrobe anyway. You're my wife now and you'll dress like it.'

Kathryn was quivering. 'I won't be bought, Logan. Please, just go away and leave me alone.'

He grasped her shoulders and hauled her up from the bed, furiously holding her in front of him with the blanket tangled between them. 'I've finally reached the end of my patience, Kathryn. You're already mine, I don't have to buy you.' His face was very close to hers and his eyes suddenly dropped to her mouth. His grip lessened and with a muffled groan he turned away from her. 'Put the coat on—now! Don't make me do it for you.'

She shuddered, wavering, then quickly wrapped herself in it before he turned back to her, his eyes twin blue flames.

'We can't go on like this.' He tried to contain his anger. 'You're fighting me at every turn. I wasn't trying to buy you—I know you better than that. You simply need some new things, and now I'm in a position to get them for you.' He raked a hand through his hair before taking a deep breath and letting it out harshly. 'We'll go home and talk like two civilised people. This is no place to do it.'

She grimaced and looked past him, not seeing the dust that lay thick on the old-fashioned dressing-table. Her eyes were blind to the faded flowers on the wallpaper and the thin worn curtains at the grimy windows. All she could see was her aunt's gentle lined face full of love and concern. This house was her refuge. This had been the only place where she had been truly happy. 'Let me stay here—please! This can be my home.'

'Are you out of your mind?' he demanded.

'I don't want to live in your house, Logan. I don't belong there.' Her eyes were huge and pleading.

'You don't know what you're saying.'

'Please, please don't make me go back!' Her voice wobbled.

Logan lost his patience again, gripping her arms in the warm coat savagely and bringing her up close to face him. 'You can't stay here. This house is in the hands of a lawyer waiting to be sold.'

'Sold?' she whispered. 'Who would dare to sell it?'

'I dare.'

'But you have no right!'

'I have every right. I took care of Miriam for months before she died. Who do you think paid for her doctor's bills, her medicine and hospital costs?' Flinty blue eyes hardened to narrow slits. 'Who do you think buried her?' he said ever so softly.

Kathryn trembled, gasping. 'Was the cost of her care so much?'

'It was enough. With the sale of her house, I should get it all back.'

'It all comes down to money with you, doesn't it? The mighty, the wealthy Logan Ramsey!' Scorn dripped from her. 'You have no right to sell this house!'

'Don't talk to me of rights, Kathryn.' He strained her closer to him, holding her in a fierce embrace. 'You're Mrs Logan Ramsey now, and I might just start demanding some of the rights that go with that name.' He tilted his dark head towards the bed. 'You were willing enough to share it last night, reaching out to me when you were so cold and lost and broken.'

'I didn't know it was you!'

'Everything changes in the cold light of day, doesn't it?' Logan sighed resignedly and let her go. 'Even though we're married, I thought we could be friends, but you insist on facing me across some kind of barrier you've erected.' He dragged in a harsh breath. 'All right, I'll respect that barrier. I won't attempt to cross it. You can tear it down all by yourself when the time is right. Come home with me now and be my son's mother. That's all I ask of you—nothing more, nothing less.'

Logan was true to his word. When they went back to his beautiful mansion set in the distant shadow of pine-strewn mountains, Kathryn became Jon's mother, not Logan's wife.

It was a completely different way of life for her

in this wildly beautiful region of British Columbia, and as winter turned into spring, she managed to relax and eventually fell into a contented routine. She even gained a few pounds and her skin bloomed with healthy colour. Jon was an undemanding child, eager to please and always grinning, sharing his childish secrets and letting her fill the empty places in his heart.

Her mornings were spent getting to know Emma Gresham, familiarising herself with the spacious house and badgering the housekeeper to let her help with at least a smattering of the housework. Her afternoons were devoted entirely to Jon, most often tramping through the lush greenery surrounding the house, discovering such delights as wildflowers and hidden violets and the spidery tracks of inquisitive animals. The immaculate rolling lawns were edged by a gurgling steam on one side and a forest teeming with wildlife on the other. And forming a spectacular backdrop behind it all were the rugged peaks of the perpetually blue Coast Range Mountains.

When Logan came home from work in the evenings, it was easy enough to escape to some other part of the house and allow him time alone with his son before Jon's bedtime. He insisted that they dine together each night, and they did so, silently, in the huge formal dining room, with Logan always looking impeccable in his exquisite dinner jackets and frilled shirts, while Kathryn sat selfconsciously proud in her hopelessly plain cotton dresses.

Only once did Logan again repeat his offer to

buy her a new wardrobe, but she sent him such a withering look that he regretted the impulse. At first his lips were tight each time he saw her in her own clothes and a small muscle jerked violently in his jaw, but lately his whole manner was changing to one of bland indifference. He didn't even seem to notice her any more. She wondered if it was all an act—and then one night she had her answer.

When their eyes happened to meet and cling across the table, she caught a look of hungry intensity in his before a shutter swiftly closed over them, effectively shutting her out. But it gave her no satisfaction to know he still desired her, even though she had defied him and refused the things he offered. He had betrayed her, and she couldn't forgive him for that. Each night when she fell into bed she would lie for hours staring at the ceiling, a terrible aching emptiness deep inside her. What she was doing to Logan wasn't fair, but what he had done to her was unforgivable.

'Kathryn?' Emma Gresham stopped her at the front door when she and Jon came in from a walk in the forest one warm afternoon towards the end of May. 'Logan rang. He won't be home for dinner again this evening.'

'Daddy's never home any more!' Jon wailed.

'It's all right, dear,' said Kathryn with a small white smile. 'Daddy's work is very important to him.' She looked at Emma. 'I suppose he had to work late? That's the classic excuse, isn't it?'

The woman's eyes filled with pity. 'That's what he said,' she murmured.

Kathryn ignored the strange pain quivering through her. 'Well then, how about all of us eating our dinner in the kitchen tonight? No sense going to the trouble of using the dining room. May we, Emma?'

'But—I've tried to make you understand. The lady of the house never eats in the kitchen. It just isn't done.'

'You should know by now I can't play the part of a lady.' Kathryn smiled ruefully and looked down at her jeans. 'I wouldn't even begin to know how. Besides, Jon and I feel more comfortable in there, don't we, Jon?'

He grinned. 'It's nice in the kitchen, and that's where you make cookies.'

Emma beamed at him, then looked at her with a small frown. 'You're nothing like your sister was,' she commented.

'You knew Carol?' Kathryn's eyes widened with surprise.

'Oh my, yes. Didn't Logan tell you? My George and I used to run this house years ago when Logan and Paul were growing up. George died about the same time as old Mrs Ramsey. I thought it was the end for me, but Logan married then and found room for me in the house he leased in Burnaby.'

'Burnaby? That's quite a way from his office.'

'I know, dear, but Logan had closed this house and Carol wanted to live there.'

'What happened to his apartment? The one in Vancouver?'

'As far as I know, he still has it, but Carol wouldn't live there. It wasn't grand enough for her.'

Kathryn swallowed. 'I—didn't know.'

'Carol was a regular——' Emma caught herself just in time. 'Jon? Will you go and check to see if I latched the back door? I was in the garden earlier and I don't remember if I closed it or not.' She watched him go, then turned back to Kathryn. 'I wouldn't dream of gossiping, you know, but your sister was difficult. Nothing was ever good enough for her. Always demanding— she'd fly into a rage at the least little thing. Logan ignored it most of the time, putting it down to her condition. When he had to work late, she never believed him. She accused him of all kinds of things.' She reached out and squeezed Kathryn's shoulder gently with a compassionate smile. 'I know there's something not quite right between the two of you and now you suspect the worst of your husband. It's there in your eyes. But if Logan tells you he had to work late, you can believe him. He's an honourable man. I've known him since he was smaller than Jon, and he'd never do that to you.'

Kathryn felt herself growing cold. 'Don't worry, Emma, I'm not about to make a scene. I've seen for myself how honourable a man Logan is.' She blinked away the picture of him and Carol in the moonlight . . .

Surprisingly, the evening passed swiftly and Kathryn decided it wouldn't hurt to let Jon stay up a little longer past his bedtime. They were in the huge drawing room and she was standing gazing through the long French windows at the fiery rays of the dying sun. Jon came to stand silently beside her, slipping his hand into hers as the sky turned from deep blue to pink and gold and purple, turning the distant mountain peaks into shimmering jewels.

'Some day I want to paint a picture, Mom,' he said in a hushed, almost reverent voice. 'In all those beautiful colours.'

'Keep the thought, Jon,' she said, smiling down at him with all her love shining in her eyes.

'That's right, son. You can do anything if you want it badly enough.'

They both jumped at the sound of Logan's deep voice, and Kathryn's face filled with a dull red stain. The way he was leaning so indolently with his shoulder against the doorjamb suggested he had been standing there for some time just watching them, and it made her squirm uncomfortably. Hard muscles rippled across his chest under a pale yellow shirt as he held out his arms to his son. His dark slacks were trim-fitting, and for the first time in months Kathryn realised he was becoming thinner.

'Daddy!' Jon flung himself into his arms and was instantly crushed in a strong warm embrace. 'I thought you had to work late.'

'I did, but I got finished sooner than I expected.'

Plainly disbelieving, Kathryn turned back to the windows, barely suppressing a shiver. What had happened to his secretary? she wondered bitterly, thinking of the beautiful blonde Margaret. How did he manage to tear himself away from his 'work'?

'Shall we build a small fire, Jon? I think your mom is cold.' He stepped close to her, lifting one eyebrow as if daring her to say something. When she made a move towards the door his eyes darkened and his nostrils flared. 'Not tonight, Kathryn. You always leave when I'm around. I want you to stay with us tonight.' Then he spoke to his son, but his eyes burned at her. 'This is a rare treat for me. I never seem to be able to spend an evening with my family any more, my work usually keeps me away, but now everything's been sorted out. It's a good thing your mother is so understanding.'

'Mom always understands,' Jon boasted. 'We get to eat with Mrs Gresham in the kitchen now since you're never home. She knows I like it in there, and Mom says she likes it better too because she doesn't have to worry she'll break anything.'

Kathryn blushed hotly and turned away from Logan's raised eyebrows in embarrassment. 'Really, Jon, I don't think your daddy's at all interested.'

'Oh, but I am.' Logan grinned broadly, setting Jon on his feet. 'Tell me more—I'm all ears!'

'Mom knocked over a vase and almost broke it when she tried to help dust in here, so Mrs Gresham told her she could help with the dishes in the kitchen instead and she wouldn't have to worry about any looms.'

'Looms?'

'That's right, isn't it, Mom?' Jon frowned.

'Heirlooms,' she said through gritted teeth.

Logan looked nonplussed, then he threw his head back and laughed deep in his throat. Walking to a low rosewood table, he pointed to a

cylindrical porcelain vase with a delicate bird
painted in blue on a twisted branch on the side of
it. Bright blue flowers surrounded the top and
deep swirls representing waves or wind completed
the picture. There were Chinese-looking symbols
at its base. 'Is this the vase?'

Jon nodded, and Kathryn stared in horrified
fascination as Logan smashed it on the floor at
his feet. They both flinched and Logan grinned
broadly. 'I've always hated that thing. Is there
anything else you're afraid to touch?'

Before they could say a word, Emma came
bustling in. 'Did I hear a crash? Oh, Kathryn!
The fifteenth-century Ming!' Her horrified eyes
flew upward. 'It was priceless!'

'Kathryn didn't break it, Emma. I did.' Logan
chuckled. 'It's something I've wanted to do for
years.'

'But you know how your mother loved it!'

'Yes, she did.' His face twisted with deep-
rooted pain. 'She loved *things*. But things don't
last, do they? When they start making a person
uncomfortable in his own home, it's time to get
rid of them.' His eyes made a quick sweep of the
beautiful room filled with sombre paintings,
heavy sculptures and vases on scattered tables,
then flickered briefly over Kathryn's strained
features. 'Pack up all these knick-knacks, Emma.
It's time we made a clean sweep of everything in
this house.'

'*Knick-knacks?*' The woman was scandalised.
'But what shall I do with them? This is priceless
art you're talking about!'

'Art belongs in a museum,' he said with a short

laugh. 'Put them in boxes and I'll give them to Paul. He might appreciate them. They don't belong here any more.'

Kathryn coloured painfully as she bent to help Emma gather up the broken bits of smashed porcelain. The sharp sting of his words went straight to her heart. She had no idea this was Ming. If she had known anything about art, she would have realised it. But she was hopelessly ignorant. Logan was right. All these things didn't belong where she wouldn't appreciate them.

After Emma had swept up the pieces and left the room muttering to herself, Kathryn sat at one end of the silk damask sofa in front of the dark marble fireplace and watched Logan explain to Jon how to place the logs to ensure a small cosy glow rather than a blazing fire. He fanned the embers, then stood and rested his forearm on the mantelpiece. Jon wanted to do the same, but he wasn't tall enough, and his mouth drooped.

'It's all right,' she told him when he came to sit by her. 'You'll grow, and one day you'll be just as tall as your daddy.'

'He's awful tall.'

'You will be too. Anyone can see that.'

Logan turned suddenly and his voice was oddly husky. 'Do you think Jon looks like me, Kathryn?'

'He's the image of you,' she said softly. 'Why do you ask?'

He shrugged his shoulders, but she could detect a strange tension about him. 'I just wondered how you saw him. Sometimes I think he has some of Carol's mannerisms, but—he's my son.' He stressed the 'my' ever so softly, and she shivered without knowing why.

'Was there ever any doubt?'

His face changed, but his eyes continued to burn with a strange intensity. 'No. Never.' He came to the sofa and lifted Jon high in his arms. 'My son! Tomorrow's a special day for you.'

'I know, Daddy,' the little boy squealed. 'Mrs Gresham told Mom and me tonight because she didn't think you'd remember. I'm going to be five. I'm growing up!'

'She was wrong to think I'd forget,' Logan said softly, holding him close. 'And as usual, your Uncle Paul is coming home too. He wanted to be sure not to miss your day.'

'Uncle Paul is nice,' Jon said with a sudden return to the solemn expression they hadn't seen in months, 'but he isn't as nice as you, Daddy.' He wiggled out of his arms and curled up beside Kathryn, clinging to her.

'What is it, Jon? Is something wrong?'

He squeezed his eyes shut and shook his head. She looked from him to Logan and back again. There was something here, but for the life of her she didn't know what it was.

'Come along, dear,' she said soothingly. 'It's past your bedtime. Give Daddy a kiss goodnight.'

He did so at once, surprising her by his ready acceptance. Kathryn noticed too that Logan had become oddly restless. She didn't understand any of the strange undercurrents that were suddenly making themselves felt in the room. When she reached the door she glanced back and saw Logan staring into the fire with his shoulders hunched forward and a curious wintry bleakness settling over his handsome face.

After settling Jon she didn't relish the thought of spending the rest of the evening in Logan's company, especially in this strange mood of his, so she slipped on a thick red sweater and silently left the house.

The air was cool and still, a full moon darting in and out of dark ribbon-like clouds, but she found her way down the path without any difficulty. She went through the garden Jon had helped Mrs Gresham plant and saw the tiny shoots beginning to poke through the soil. Walking towards a slight hill far from the house, she looked up at a row of huge pine trees silvery in the moonlight. Her face was lifted past them towards the evening sky and she closed her eyes, letting the peace and tranquillity wash over her. She stood quite still for a long time lost in a star-spangled silence as the moonlight played over her. Unbidden, thoughts of Logan filled her mind. But this time it was not the picture of him and Carol she saw. It was herself with him, and suddenly her eyes flew open in alarm. When had she started to think like that? She swallowed and wrapped her arms around herself, trying to suppress a shudder. Don't let me love him again, she prayed. Love means loss and betrayal and unbearable pain.

Logan wasn't really her husband. A few words spoken by a judge didn't mean anything. Their names signed to a certificate didn't make a marriage. It was what was in their hearts that counted. And she would keep her heart closed to him.

'So you enjoy nights like these, too?' Logan said softly, coming to stand behind her so quietly that she jumped violently. 'I didn't mean to frighten you.'

'I—I didn't hear you coming,' she gulped.

'I'm sure if you had, you'd have disappeared,' he said dryly.

Kathryn tried to move past him, but he caught her by the shoulders and turned her towards him.

'Don't go—please!' His voice was thick with emotion and her heart began to pound in her throat as she tried to shake off his hands.

'We really don't have anything to say to each other.' Her fingers tried to prise his hands loose, but he only seemed amused by her attempt to free herself. With deliberately slow movements he lowered his head and his mouth was unbearably gentle as his lips found hers. He easily drew her stiffly resisting body in a close embrace, and she willed herself not to give in to this gentle insistence. If she remained passive surely he would leave her alone.

His fingers tangled in her hair and he moulded her body closer to his solid strength. His lips were firm and warm as their breath mingled, and all at once Kathryn felt her traitorous body succumbing to his subtle demands. Passion flared between them, coursing through her in a hungry wave, and this apparent loss of control frightened her and she struggled against him, fighting her own desire as much as his.

'Don't, please,' she moaned against his mouth.

Logan continued to hold her close against him, but the quality of his kiss suddenly changed and became insulting as he demanded more of her. His fingers tightened in her hair as he grabbed a handful and dragged her head back to look her full in the face. His cold blue eyes glinted like hard steel. 'You're mine,' he said. 'You and Jon. My wife and my son.' His voice was unnaturally quiet as he hissed through tight jaws: 'Neither of you will ever leave me.'

'What are you talking about?' she gasped.

Before she realised what he was about to do, his fingers grasped the neck of her blouse and she heard the thin material rip, then he slipped his hand inside, cupping her breast.

'I want you, Kathryn,' he muttered. His voice changed then, became cajoling as he stroked her with long warm fingers. 'Let me love you. How can you pretend you don't want me? Do you think I can't feel what your body is telling me? Remember how it used to be all that time ago? Your eyes and your body promised me heaven, promised me everything. I could have taken you any time. But now——'

'Logan—*please!*' She was horrified by the pleasurable senations running through her. She should have been repulsed, but he knew exactly what he was doing. A fine tingling feathered along her spine. He was a master at seduction. He must have known many women, not just her sister. The picture of him and Carol flashed again in her mind, bringing her back to her senses, and she struggled against him.

He jerked her head back roughly and she cried out in appalling pain as once again his lips, no longer gentle, took hers in a savage plunder, his hunger insatiable. Her mouth was bruised and all at once she could taste the warm sticky wetness of blood.

Her head was throbbing and she winced with pain when he finally let her go. She stepped back, staggering, trembling, her arms crossed in front of her in an effort to cover her breasts.

When Logan recovered himself he had the grace to look ashamed. His stood with his face averted, his hands at his sides, his breathing ragged. 'I'm sorry. I promised myself I wouldn't touch you until you came to me. I don't know why tonight——' He hesitated before adding: 'It won't happen again.'

Kathryn stood there with the heavy weight of her hair tangled in black disorder about her shoulders, a thin trickle of blood at her lips, her arms crossed in front of her, and Logan's eyes took on a glacial bleakness as he bowed his head and strode away in the direction of his house, leaving her looking at his powerful retreating back.

To her horror, a breathless yearning shivered through her and she knew that all he had to do was turn around and ask her to come to him and she would be his. She'd be whatever he wanted her to be, would do whatever he asked. He had given her every cause to hate him, but her treacherous heart betrayed her. All those years away from him didn't even begin to kill her love for him as she wanted them to. They merely intensified it.

'I can't love him. I can't. Oh, Logan!' she moaned over and over. Her whispers were lost in the stillness of the trees.

CHAPTER FIVE

Jon's birthday dawned bright and clear and warm, and when Kathryn looked in on him, he giggled mischievously from his bed.

'Happy birthday, darling,' she smiled, coming to sit beside him. 'I found something I thought you'd like to have.'

He scrambled from beneath the covers and, kneeling, wound his arms about her neck, laughing and embracing her. His face was warm and rosy, his black hair tousled from sleep. Planting a warm kiss on her cheek, he drew a little away from her and looked down at the small stuffed animal in her hands. It was a bear, not a new one, for one ear had been meticulously mended several times and the fur was worn in places, but it was obviously well loved.

'It was in the box of things your dad collected from Aunt Miriam's house for me,' Kathryn said with a small pang, remembering. 'This little bear came with us all the way from England when Aunt Miriam brought Carol and me to Canada to live with her. It was your mother's favourite thing.'

'You mean you had it when you were little like me?' Jon looked at the bear with shining eyes and held it reverently, missing the look of chagrin that ran across her face. He had misunderstood. A sudden sharp spasm of pain went through her and she knew she should tell him it was Carol's, not hers, just as he was Carol's son, not hers. But all at once a lump lodged in her throat and all she could do was swallow hard and gather him in her arms. *Oh, Carol, your son is mine, isn't he?*

As if Jon realised there was something else here, he clung to her and murmured softly: 'Thank you, Mom. It'll be my favourite too. I'll take care of him just like you did.'

It was a golden moment for the two of them in the big sunny bedroom done in shades of brilliant yellow deepening into beige and brown and burnt orange. The spread covering the narrow single bed was of umber silk matching the soft pile of the carpeting, and behind them were shelves with books and toy cars and wooden building blocks on them, and a big cork board on which Jon had pinned several crayon drawings of stick people representing Kathryn and his father and himself.

An invisible thread of love stretched from her heart to his, binding them together, and all at once she found it so very easy to forgive her sister and Logan for what she had seen that hot August night so long ago. This child had been the result of that union—she was sure of it. The bitterness of betrayal left her, and she looked at Jon with swimming eyes and a swelling heart and silently thanked Carol for him. 'I love you, my son,' she said softly.

Jon got up then and dressed in jeans and a bright blue shirt, and together they went downstairs to find Emma.

'Happy birthday, Jon,' she said, smiling at him from the kitchen doorway. 'I'll have breakfast ready shortly, but you'll have to have it in the morning room today. Your dad's in there waiting for you.'

Jon raced away, and Kathryn followed him more sedately, trying to ignore her sudden quickened heartbeat and the tensing of her stomach.

In place of his usual business suit, he was wearing slim-fitting Levi's and hiking boots and a blue checked shirt. The novelty of seeing him at that time of the morning held both Kathryn and Jon speechless. Usually he was gone before they were awake.

'Happy birthday, Jon.' He hugged his son briefly and merely nodded coolly to Kathryn, then turned back to the table and a nearly empty coffee cup. If he remembered what happened between them last night he didn't show it.

Jon beamed at his father and his eyes danced. 'Are you staying home today, Daddy?'

His face softened involuntarily. 'I have to make a few phone calls later to check with Margaret— but yes, I intend to spend the day with you. That's why I've been working late all these nights—so I could take some time off and not feel guilty about neglecting the business.' He flicked an eyebrow in Kathryn's direction as she took a place at the table.

She looked up with a start. Oh, how she wanted to believe that! He hadn't been living it up with Margaret as she so jealously imagined. Her heart thumped and she couldn't stop the blood from singing in her veins. 'Jon and I planned a picnic in the woods today,' she said in a small husky voice. 'Is that all right with you?'

Logan turned the full force of an ice-blue gaze on her, roaming over her hesitant smile, then falling to her faded once-red gingham blouse and patched jeans. 'You're not dressed for anything else. It's always some type of solitary outdoor excursion for you, isn't it?'

The coldness of his voice shattered the air and she couldn't control the sudden flush of embarrassment sweeping over her, but she did manage to keep from making even more of a fool of herself by stiffening her shoulders and biting her lip rather than saying anything more. The rebuke was fitting. She had been a proud fool, rejecting the clothing he bought for her. The few things she had were a disgrace to him and an embarrassment. Why hadn't she admitted it before? All at once she wanted him to see her dressed in something beautiful. But with a sinking feeling, she knew it wouldn't make any difference now. The damage had been done. She still had her pride, but at what cost?

'Can we have a picnic, Daddy?' Jon wiggled in his chair, nearly upsetting his orange juice. 'This is going to be the best birthday I ever had!'

Kathryn reached out to put a restraining hand on his shoulder, but stopped with it in mid-air. A loud commotion came from the front of the house. A car horn was blaring and there was loud shouting. Whoever was ringing the doorbell kept his finger pressed against the button so long that the chimes set up a loud protesting discordant din. Her eyes flew to Logan in alarm, but he sat quite still as if he didn't hear a thing out of the ordinary.

'That'll be Paul,' he said with a smothered sigh. 'It's part of his image to make an entrance. Shall we go and welcome the prodigal son?' He pushed back his chair and started around the table.

A frown crossed Kathryn's face when she saw Jon cowering in his chair, and a sharp sense of calamity began to feather along her spine. 'What's the matter?' she asked gently.

He pressed his little white face into her side and clung to her. 'I forgot he was coming. I don't want to see him.'

'Jon!' She was shocked. 'Why not?'

He was trembling, and she looked up to Logan for an answer, but he looked right through her.

'I told you before,' he said harshly, 'you don't have to be afraid of your uncle.' His face was set in rigid lines as he stepped close, gathering Jon up in his strong arms, holding him tightly, protectively. 'You know your mother and I would never let anyone or anything harm you.' He threw a challenging look to Kathryn, daring her to deny it.

'But you're not my father!' Jon blurted out. 'Uncle Paul said he was. And he said the next time he came home he was going to take me away from you!'

Stunned, Kathryn could only gape at him in horror.

Logan gripped Jon hard and looked straight into his face. His own was dark with rage. 'He told you that before he left on his last tour?'

Jon nodded, and bravely wiped his eyes with the backs of his hands.

'Then you should have come to me instead of keeping it to yourself. I would have tried to help you understand what he meant. You were too young before, but you're older now and you must listen to me. It was a practical joke—and not a very funny one. Uncle Paul was only trying to tease you. Whatever else you believe, I'm your father. I am—do you hear me? And when I married Kathryn, she became you mother. No one can change that.'

Kathryn stared at them, not knowing what to think. Hesitating only an instant, she wrapped her arms around both of them so Jon was securely between them. 'Your daddy's right, Jon,' she whispered reassuringly. 'You're our son. You'll live here with us always and we'll never let anyone take you away from us. What would we do without you? Who would we go on picnics with if we didn't have you?'

Logan's eyes flickered when he looked at her over the top of his son's head. They widened, then flashed with a brilliant blue questioning spark. He opened his mouth to say something, but Jon let out a small relieved breath and spoke first. 'You really mean it, Mom?'

'Jon,' she said sternly in mock reproof but tempering it with a smile, 'I wouldn't lie to you and neither would your father. Ever.' Maybe it wasn't fair to say it with so much conviction, since she didn't really know what this was all about, but Jon's peace of mind was most important right now.

He gave her a watery smile and looked up at Logan. 'Then I don't have to go with Uncle Paul even if he says so?'

'Your uncle only wishes he had a son like you,' he said through his teeth, his face suddenly a sick grey. 'But he's not your father, and he had no right to tell you he'd take you away from me. We'll go and say hello and welcome him back—but you're our son and you'll always stay with us. Remember that.'

Jon blinked and shot them a wide relieved smile, accepting what he said with a sublime innocence before Logan set him on his feet. They each took one tiny hand and stood looking at each other in a long and eloquent silence. Kathryn was teeming with a hundred questions, but she knew they would have to wait. This was no time for explanations.

The racket had stopped by the time they reached the front hall and she saw Paul in the open doorway with his back to them, snapping out instructions to a uniformed chauffeur. He was much the same height and as thin as Logan was now, and he moved with an easy indolent grace as his hands swept the air with a flourish. He was wearing a dark blue suit that fitted his lean body to perfection all the way from his straight broad shoulders to the backs of his gleaming black shoes. Kathryn noticed his hair was a rich velvety black, sparsely flecked with silver just like Logan's. They must be near the same age, she thought for a fleeting moment, then Paul dismissed his chauffeur and turned to them.

All at once the floor rocked beneath her feet.

All her breath left her in a rush and her heart began to roar in her ears. Ice raced up and down her spine in thin shuddering trickles, making her hair stand on end. All the colour drained from her face. She became rigid. Her mouth opened soundlessly and she gasped as her senses whirled.

Paul was thin but with more of a delicate leanness in place of Logan's hard muscularity, his face was unlined and colourless compared to Logan's swarthy tan, but there was no denying that the man standing in front of her oozing a practised oily charm was Logan's twin. Identical! Exact replicas of each other! She looked from one to the other in astonishment. Never had she seen two people look so much alike. Both were tall and broad. Both wore their wavy black hair stylishly long. Both had the same handsome face she loved.

So many things began to crowd into her mind: the bright glowing silver of moonlight, the scent of pine, the warm breeze of a remembered August night, dimly flashing bodies, the soft whisper of loving sounds. They began to spin, whirl, buzz through her head. Then she came back to the present with a start and saw Logan standing in front of her, staring oddly, and she heard Paul speaking.

'Happy birthday, son,' he said with a mocking smile glittering in his eyes. He ran a long-fingered hand across Jon's cheek before turning to Kathryn, ignoring Logan altogether. 'And who might this lovely lady be?' His blue eyes held a wicked glint when they stopped briefly on her mouth before sliding appreciatively over the

gentle swell of her breasts straining against the
faded gingham blouse to her slim waist and
narrow hips in patched jeans.

'This is my mom,' said Jon in a clear voice, but
he gripped her hand so tightly she felt it tingle.

Paul's eyes narrowed thoughtfully. 'I see. Just
one big happy family, eh?' He reached out and
took her ice-cold hand, kissing it in a grand
manner that made her skin crawl. 'How do you
do, sister-in-law?'

A hectic colour ran into her face, but she
managed to keep her breathless voice controlled.
'Logan never told me you were a twin.'

'Didn't he?' He turned to his brother and she
snatched her hand away from his caressing
fingers with an instinctive aversion. 'You're
slipping, old boy.' Underneath his suave charm
she sensed a ruthless steel core, and the studied
quietness of his next words confirmed it. 'If you
think your having a wife makes any difference to
my fight to claim Jon, you're sadly mistaken.' He
looked again at Kathryn. 'Now why didn't my
brother think to tell you he's a twin, I wonder?'

'I think of you only as a brother, not a twin,
Paul. That should answer your question.' Logan
inclined his head coolly and looked at Kathryn
in a strangely searching way, then lifted his
shoulders with irritation. 'You're just in time for
breakfast. Let's not keep Emma waiting any
longer. Kathryn? Paul?' He lifted Jon in his arms
and stepped away from the doorway to let them
precede him.

Paul put his arm out to her in a cavalier motion
and Kathryn willed herself not to recoil from his

touch. There was no reason for this aversion to him. He looked so much like Logan, yet there was a disturbing difference somehow. She kept staring at him, unable to look away. A twin! Could she have been mistaken all those years ago? Had it been *Paul* with Carol? A shudder ran through her. If that was true, why was he so insistent that Jon was his son?

Paul looked deeply into her eyes as if searching for something, and then all he said was: 'Ah—h—h,' as if inordinately satisfied.

By the time Jon had polished off his birthday breakfast of pancakes and sausages, he had regained some of his usual good spirits and sat very much at ease close to Kathryn in the bright sunny room. If anyone noticed her preoccupation or her lack of appetite or how she kept looking uncomfortably from one brother to the other, they didn't mention it.

'So. What have you planned for today?' asked Paul, leaning back in his chair, pushing away his coffee cup and idly tipping an ash from his cigarette into a heavy crystal ashtray. His eyes flicked over their casual clothing before he gave an expressive shudder. 'Something rustic?'

'We're going on a picnic,' Logan said shortly. 'I don't expect you'll want to come along.'

'A picnic?' Paul raised his black eyebrows and Kathryn felt his silent mocking laughter. 'How—quaint! I should have expected as much from an uncivilised brute like you—but how did you manage to talk your lovely wife into it? She doesn't look the outdoor type.'

'It was my idea, Paul,' she cut in, coming to

Logan's defence. 'Jon particularly likes the forest, but we don't allow him to go there alone. I thought it would be nice to spend the day letting him explore.'

His eyes flashed. 'Trying to make a lumberman out of him? It won't work, you know. He's his father's son.'

'Yes, he's very like Logan,' she said sweetly through her teeth. 'How clever of you to recognise that.' Ignoring both his and Logan's look of surprise at this rudeness, she stood and rested her hands on Jon's shoulders. 'If you'll excuse us, Paul? Logan?' She smiled a particularly warm smile at her husband and got a small questioning frown in return. 'Jon and I promised to help Mrs Gresham get the picnic basket ready. Did you say you were joining us, Paul?'

He nodded petulantly. 'I wouldn't miss this for the world!'

For nearly an hour Paul kept them waiting while he tried to find something suitable to wear. He came into the kitchen grumbling loudly about not having his valet to help him co-ordinate his clothing. 'But he'll be here tomorrow, with the rest of my entourage,' he promised.

'You look fine.' Kathryn managed to keep a straight face when she saw his stark white slacks, white shirt and spotless white shoes.

'All set, Paul?' Logan came in and looked him up and down.

'How do I look?' He spread his arms and did a small turn for them.

Kathryn's eyes widened and Jon frowned before leaning against her side, but Logan managed to keep a grin contained and merely looked thoughtful. 'You'll do,' he said. 'At least we don't have to worry about you getting lost.'

Paul studied his face suspiciously but couldn't detect any sarcasm. It went right over his head. 'Good. If we're all ready, then, let's go. Emma? I hope you've included some of my favourites in that delicious basket?' He rubbed his hands delicately and gave her a charming smile.

'Of course,' the little woman beamed. 'Fried chicken, cole slaw, fresh baked rolls. I remembered some white wine and when I packed the strawberry tarts, I put in an extra one just for you.'

'Ah! Trust you to remember.' He bent over her hand and tried to kiss it, but she raised it sharply, hitting him square on his nose.

'Oh! I'm so sorry, Paul!' she said innocently when he jerked himself bolt upright. 'Did I hurt you?'

A thin trickle of blood slithered down to his lip before he rubbed his fingers gingerly over his nose. His face was a study in horror when he took away his hand and saw the red stain on his fingertips.

Kathryn gasped and barely held back a guffaw before hustling Jon out of the back door. If she stayed, she'd make an absolute fool of herself! A gurgle started in her throat and the more she tried to hold it in, the more she wanted to laugh. When Logan followed her outside, grinning from ear to ear, it was her undoing. She sank to her knees, reeling with mirth, laughing uproariously.

'Did you see the look on his face?' Logan slapped his thigh, letting out a loud whoop.

'I think Emma did that on purpose,' she said, wiping tears from her eyes.

Jon frowned and looked from one to the other. 'Mom? Daddy? Why are you laughing?'

Logan reached for Kathryn and helplessly pulled her against his broad chest before gathering Jon close in the warm circle too. 'Something just struck us as funny, Jon.'

'It struck Paul too,' she said, and that set them laughing all over again.

It took a good five minutes for them to regain their composure, but when Paul came out of the house sporting an ice-pack he didn't really need, they started again.

'Come on, Jon,' said Kathryn with a strangled gurgle. 'I'll race you to the woods!'

Logan suddenly developed a throaty cough that took some time to stop.

'You really should see about that cough, old boy,' Paul said with a muffled nasally sound that made him cough all the harder.

Kathryn was still laughing when they crossed the lawn and made their way into the cool green forest. Logan led the way, carrying the picnic basket easily while hacking out a path without destroying any of the trees. For almost half an hour they walked single file through pine-scented greenness. Twigs snapped and crunched under their feet, leaves rustled and birds sent up a raucous din protesting against the intrusion into their sanctuary.

Every once in a while Logan would point out something of interest: the peculiar growth of a tree twisting towards a patch of sunlight or a bright-feathered bird hidden in the deep branches of a pine. He took the time to explain why the forest was a necessary part of nature and made it a vivid exciting story rather than a boring lecture on conservation. His voice was deep and vibrant, and Kathryn felt a tingling sensation all along her spine whenever he spoke. Several times they had to wait for Paul to catch up to them, and once when he was quite far behind, she took the opportunity to sit on a fallen tree trunk and catch her breath.

'Tired?' asked Logan in a quiet soothing voice, his eyes glittering in his handsome face.

She leaned back on her elbows, letting the heavy weight of her hair trail on the log behind her. 'No, not tired. Just—content.'

'Content?' He came to sit beside her while Jon was searching for pine cones several yards away. 'That's the last thing I'd expect you to say. I'd have thought you'd be full of curiosity, wanting the answers to a hundred different questions about my brother and why he says he's Jon's father.'

'I am curious, but I'm sure you aren't able to enlighten me now. I hope there'll be time when we get back home?' Her heart pounded as he leaned closer, searching her face for something. She was mesmerised by the intense blue of his eyes and her mind whirled, wanting to ask, to explain, to clarify that haunting picture always in her thoughts. Which of them had she seen? Who was really Jon's father? Yet how could she come right out and ask such a thing?

'You're the most unusual woman I've ever

known,' Logan said softly, hesitantly. His hands curved on either side of her neck lightly caressing the wildly throbbing pulse beating against his fingers before pulling her against him, his eyes darkening with emotion. His thumbs stroked her chin gently, forcing her face up. His mouth made a tentative descent and when she didn't protest or turn away, his lips fastened on hers, warm and firm and infinitely gentle.

Her arms began to circle his back and all at once she gripped his hard flesh through the thin material of his shirt, clinging to him as her mouth instinctively opened to the helpless driving possession of his.

His fingers tangled in the silky length of her hair, arching her slender neck, making the glowing embers she had tried to keep hidden flare to life, trembling through her, melting her bones. She was pliant clay willing to be moulded into whatever he wanted her to be.

When he reluctantly drew his mouth away from her and lifted his head, she opened her eyes and gazed into his. They were impossible to read.

'Kathryn, I——'

'*Where are you?*' Paul's strident voice cut through the stillness, shattering the moment between them. They heard him crashing through the underbrush and Logan muttered an oath deep in his throat.

'Over here, Paul. To your left.'

Kathryn shivered, missing the comforting warmth of Logan's body as he pulled away from her. Why did he have to come just at this moment? It was full of promise, and she felt she was on the verge of discovering something wonderful. It was as if they suddenly had been transported back in time and the past five years had never happened.

Logan looked at her with a silent question and his eyes glittered before he stood up, rubbing the back of his neck as if he would like to do violence to his brother. 'It's not much farther,' he muttered, watching Paul carefully pick his way towards them. His lip curled when he saw him step lightly around a moss-covered rock, vainly trying not to get his shoes dirty.

'Remember how father used to drag us here every Saturday, old boy?' said Paul, taking out a white silk handkerchief to wipe his face and hands. 'Always talking about how the Indians taught him how to survive in the Yukon? I hated it then and I hate it even more now. Did you have to come so far?'

'You had the choice to stay home,' Logan said shortly. 'The clearing's just ahead. Come on, Jon.' Without waiting to let Paul catch his breath, he held back a thick low branch so they could continue on. It started to slip from his grasp and for a moment Kathryn thought he was going to let it snap back at Paul, but he held it long enough for all of them to pass.

'This place has nothing but distressing memories for me,' Paul complained. 'Not only did I have to come here with you and Father and learn about forestry, but this also happens to be the place where Mary Lou proposed to me.'

Kathryn looked back in surprise. 'You're married, Paul?'

He grimaced. 'Mary Lou was my first wife. Quite a domineering outdoor type—a horsey woman, if you know what I mean. I honestly did try to understand her love for the wide open spaces, but then I met Theresa and that was that.'

Her jaw dropped and Logan raised his eyebrows wryly, smiling at her surprise. 'Paul's had three wives so far. Mary Lou, Theresa and— what was the name of the other one?'

'Connie,' Paul said shortly. 'She was the smartest of the lot. I have to pay her more alimony than the other two combined. Quite a pair, aren't we, old boy?' He shook his head, laughing as if at a huge joke. 'I've had three and you've had two. Do you think it's some kind of record?'

Kathryn turned away abruptly, trying not to let them see how sickened she was by Paul's easy smiles and coarse laughter. Marriage wasn't a game. How could he find it so easy to marry and then decide that his wife was not the right one after all? And then she thought of the ease with which Logan had married her and a sudden pain flickered in her eyes. It wouldn't do to start thinking like that, start jumping to conclusions. She put it out of her mind and shuddered, picking her way blindly down a slope that ended in a beautiful bright green clearing with a small stream rippling over shiny pebbles.

Here the sunlight was nearly blinding after the deep gloom of the forest and it gave the moss-covered ground a dappled brilliance that was warmly inviting. She stood blinking and shook her head in awe. 'It's beautiful,' she whispered.

Jon was delighted and promptly sat down to take off his shoes and socks and wade through the crystal-clear water.

'No, Jon!' Both Kathryn and Logan spoke together, then looked at each other.

'What's the harm in it?' queried Paul.

'The stones are sharp and the water's a lot colder than you think,' Logan said shortly setting the picnic basket on a rock out of the way. He turned to his son. 'Later on in the summer I'll let you swim with me in the lake.' Putting an affectionate arm across his shoulders, he smiled at him. 'Let's go explore. Your mother and uncle look like they could use a rest. They'll be all right till we come back.'

It was much warmer here in the sun, and Kathryn took off the sweater she wore over her blouse and settled down on the grassy bank trailing her fingers in the water. Paul merely stood shifting uncomfortably from one foot to the other.

'Er—would you mind if I used your sweater?'

She frowned over her shoulder at him standing so ill at ease. 'It'll probably be too small—but go ahead.'

'I don't want to wear it. I want to sit on it.' He wrinkled his nose and smoothed his hands down the sides of his white pants.

'Of course,' she breathed, 'I should have realised you'd need something. It's an old one that's seen better days, so go ahead and use it.' She wasn't about to tell him it was the only one she had.

'Thanks.' Paul looked at it as if it wasn't good

enough to sit on, then settled himself quite close to her and stretched out his long legs before lighting a cigarette. Smoke curled above his head and Kathryn couldn't take her eyes off him. He looked so much like Logan it was unreal. 'You have a kind heart, my dear,' he smiled. 'Anyone can see it at a glance.'

She looked at him warily, recognising the practised charm and trying not to let it bother her.

He continued to smile at her, ignoring her faint shudders. 'Forgive me if this seems a bit trite, but haven't I seen you somewhere before? Ever since breakfast this morning I've been trying to place you. There's something so—familiar—about your face.'

Something inside her quivered. 'Don't you know?'

'Know? Know what?'

'Carol was my sister.'

He sat bolt upright and stared hard at her. 'No! You're not *that* Kathryn! Logan spent half a million dollars looking for you—and you're Carol's sister. What was he thinking? How could he be so crass? Don't you mind taking Carol's place?'

Her face hardened. 'I have my own place, Paul. Carol has nothing to do with it.'

'Carol has everything to do with it. She had my son! Logan took him away from me and now he's put you in her place.'

Kathryn shuddered. 'I didn't know Carol knew you.'

'Oh? Well, I suppose she wouldn't have said

anything. I was married at the time and we had to keep our affair a secret. Then Logan stepped in and married her and put a stop to it.'

She swallowed hard as jagged pieces of the puzzle kept falling into place. Logan told her he hadn't chosen Carol. She was there, he said. She was there and she was pregnant, and he had to do the honourable thing and marry her to give Jon the Ramsey name. Ice trickled down her spine. And she had condemned him . . .

Paul knelt close to her. 'Help me, Kathryn. You know Jon's mine—I can see it in your eyes. Carol and I had something wonderful going for us before Logan stepped in. She was the only one able to give me a child, but my brother married her and pretends he's his.' His beautiful blue eyes flashed darkly, reminding her so much of Logan. 'You know it's true, I can see it in your face. Jon's mine and I want him back.'

'No——'

His hands fastened on her shoulders to give her a shake, but he lost his balance and fell heavily on top of her, knocking the breath from her lungs. 'Why should Logan have him? He's got everything else I've ever wanted. My father's will gave him control of the company and our beautiful home is in his name. Even my half of the Ramsey fortune is in a trust fund under his control until I'm forty. I won't let him have my son too!'

'You don't know what you're saying!' she gasped, trying to twist her slim body away from him. But he pinned her to the ground.

'You can help me if you try. I know it must bother you to look at Jon and see Carol in him.

He's a constant reminder of her. Do you ever look at him and think of Logan and Carol lying together? If you help me, I'll take him away and you'll never have to see him again.'

'Get away from me!' she gasped, horrified by what he was saying. She heaved against him, trying to push him off her but he was much too heavy. 'You're hurting me!'

'Just think of how much Logan's hurting me,' Paul said shrilly. 'I'm that boy's father, but he won't admit it.'

Kathryn looked up at him with wide strained eyes. Somehow she had to get away from him. 'Please, Paul . . . I can't breathe!'

'Then stop fighting me.' When she stopped struggling and lay still, he rolled most of his heavy weight off her but kept her pinned to the soft ground, digging his fingers painfully into the smooth flesh of her wrists, lifting them above her head, keeping one long leg entwined with hers. 'Promise me you'll help and I'll let you up,' he said softly.

Her heart hammered in her throat and her mind raced. 'There's nothing I can do.'

'Oh yes, there is, old girl. I'll show you what to do.' He swooped forward to plant a warm wet kiss on her lips, but she twisted her head away and jerked violently when her distended eyes saw Logan's blue jean-clad legs and thick hiking boots on the ground right beside her.

'What's all this?' he demanded with brutal savagery, standing with his feet planted firmly apart, his hands on his hips, cold fury in every line of his rigid body.

A guilty red surged to her face as Paul rolled easily to his feet and smoothed his rumpled clothes. He didn't bother helping her up but looked at several grass stains on his knees and began daintily brushing himself down.

'I seem to have made a mess of these slacks, haven't I?' he said with a light laugh.

Logan's face congested with murderous rage as he roughly pulled Kathryn up from the ground. 'And I seem to have come back just in time,' he grated. 'If you have no consideration for me, at least you could have thought of Jon. What do you think he'd do if he saw you like this?'

All the colour drained from her face. 'It isn't what you think! We were just——'

'That's enough!' he thundered. 'I don't want to hear it. I have eyes and I can see.'

She stiffened and looked past him to Paul, who was still fussing with his slacks. A small smirk played about his mouth, and a terrible pain struck at her when she realised she had played right into his hands. Any closeness that might have developed between her and Logan was over. He had jumped to the obvious conclusion—just as she had more than five years before. 'Oh, Logan, don't make the same mistake I did!' Her mouth trembled and she put her hand on his arm, but he pulled harshly away from her.

Jon came running up just then and stopped abruptly, clutching a handful of bright wild-flowers in front of him. 'I picked the flowers like you said, Daddy. Mom? Why is your hair full of pine needles?' He looked from her to his father and then to Paul. 'Your pants are all dirty, Uncle Paul. Did you fall?'

'You could say that, son. I know a lot of men who would fall for your mother.' Paul laughed lightly and stepped to the picnic basket. 'Are you about ready to eat? I'm famished.'

Kathryn flung herself away from all of them and wished the ground would open up and swallow her. But nothing could be that easy. Jon came to stand in front of her frowning with solemn eyes.

'Daddy said these flowers looked like you, fragile but full of fire. What's fragile, Mom?'

Her eyes filled. 'It means easily broken.'

He stared up at her. 'I wouldn't let anybody break you.'

'I know you wouldn't.' She dropped to her knees and took the flowers, putting her arms around him. 'Thank you, darling. It's so good to know I have a protector. It's your birthday but here you are, giving me presents. They're beautiful.'

'Daddy said a present was going to be delivered for me today, but it didn't come before we left. What do you think it is?' Jon's eyes glowed with anticipation.

'We'll just have to wait and see, won't we?' Kathryn looked past him to Logan, who stood with his hands on his hips, staring bleakly at her.

CHAPTER SIX

THE rest of the afternoon went from bad to worse. Whenever Kathryn had a moment alone with Jon, Logan was right there beside her, listening intently to their slightest conversation. As if she would say anything to endear Paul to him, she thought despairingly, sickened by Paul's smirks and feigned unawareness of what was happening. Logan no longer trusted her and was making it painfully obvious. So many times she looked at him with a silent plea for understanding, but something flashing in his bitter blue eyes told her it was pointless. His mind was closed to her— just as hers had been to him all those years ago. When she had seen him with Carol she hadn't waited around for an explanation. Her trust had been shattered. Oh, the irony of it!

Late in the afternoon Jon fell asleep in her lap, and for one poignant moment she held him in her arms like a baby, loving the way his lashes lay on his cheeks like long black fans. Logan watched her grimly, then with a cold protective fierceness snatched him away from her with a curt command that it was time to leave.

'Protective devil, isn't he?' Paul murmured consolingly, watching the colour come and go in Kathryn's face as she got to her feet and bent to gather up the picnic basket. 'Let me carry that for you, my dear,' he said with a gallant bow, his fingers caressing hers when he took it from her.

She shuddered, but there was no way she could avoid his touch without dropping it and spilling everything. Glancing quickly at Logan, she saw his face harden and with a guilty crimson blush knew he had seen the exchange and misconstrued it.

Coldly, he turned away and ordered them to follow him.

Jon was held easily in his arms and slept all during the long silent walk back through the woods. The outing had started with such promise, but how different everything was now, Kathryn sighed.

As they neared the house Jon woke and blinked bemusedly, then grinned at Emma who was standing at the back door. 'It was super, just like you said it would be.'

'Well, I'm glad somebody had a good time,' she said, looking slightly harassed. 'But I have to say I'm glad your birthday only comes once a year, young man. If one more delivery truck comes ...' Her breath left her in a rush of exasperation.

His eyes sparkled. 'My present came?'

'Present? It's a wonder there's anything left in the toy stores for all the other children in the country,' she tutted as Logan set him on his feet.

'What are you talking about?' questioned Logan, taking the picnic basket from Paul and setting it on the scrubbed butcher block countertop in the kitchen. 'I didn't order any toys.'

'I did, old boy,' said Paul with a selfconscious laugh. 'Jon's birthday is special to me too. After all, I am——'

Logan cut him off with a look. 'I told you before——'

'And I told you,' Paul broke in coldly, taking a challenging stance, 'I have every right to buy him things. He's my——'

'Nephew!' Logan grated with a daunting expression. The steely quietness of the word sent a shiver down Kathryn's spine. 'And don't you ever forget it.'

'Oh, look!' Jon turned and ran across the shiny red tiles to a wicker basket with a perky yellow bow on its side. 'Oh, Mom! It's a dog!' His face was full of wonder and Kathryn was grateful for the diversion. They looked ready to come to blows.

She crossed the room and dropped to her knees beside Jon to admire the German shepherd puppy. His coat was a warm shade of beige with distinguished black markings running all the way from his nose to his furiously wagging tail.

Jon's eyes nearly popped out of his head when he put out a tentative hand to pet him. 'He's so soft,' he whispered.

'Pet him gently, Jon.' Logan came to stand beside them and spoke with quiet authority. 'We couldn't have a pet where we lived before, but now that we're here, there's all the room you need for him to run and play with you.'

When Kathryn gathered up the puppy to show Jon how to hold him, his wet pink tongue licked her face, and Jon giggled, pressing himself close to her.

Paul watched them and shuddered delicately. 'A dog? Messy things, aren't they?'

'It all depends on how you look at it.' Logan looked him coldly up and down. 'Drago wasn't messy.'

Paul's eyebrows rose in surprise. 'Are you talking about the same Drago I remember? He was always at our heels. He chewed up my shoes, clawed my clothes, ruined everything he could get his grubby paws on!'

'That's not what I remember about him. He was a friend.'

'Maybe to you but not to me. It was a relief when Mother finally got rid of him.'

'She was quite ruthless when it came to that, wasn't she?' Logan said conversationally, but there was a flash of deep-rooted pain in his eyes.

'Do you blame her? After all, he'd just broken her new Sèvres urn. She went to a lot of trouble and expense at that auction, and the very day she brought it home, he broke it.'

'You had a dog, Daddy?' asked Jon, looking up at him with a flicker of sympathetic understanding far beyond his years.

'Yes. My father brought him home when Uncle Paul and I were ten. He was a big dog, a German shepherd too.'

'I like this little one.' Jon threw his arms around his father's legs. 'Thank you, Daddy! Can I call him Drago too? I like that name.'

'Drago it is,' Logan smiled, squatting on the floor and putting an arm around him. He never looked at Kathryn. His unreadable eyes stayed on the puppy wriggling in her arms.

'Well, I think I'll shower and change while you three make fools of yourselves over that dog,' Paul muttered resentfully. 'Maybe when I'm finished Jon will find the time to see what I bought for him.'

Kathryn was the first to realise how rude that would be. She set the puppy gently back in his basket and looked at Jon. 'We really shouldn't slight your uncle.'

Paul nodded, ignoring Logan's tight-lipped silence, and then turned to Emma standing at the sink. 'Where are Jon's things?'

'They're in his room,' she said. 'I didn't know where else to put them.'

'Very well,' he smiled, rubbing his hands in anticipation. 'Come along, son.'

Jon dragged his feet as he followed Paul. He kept looking back to the basket where Drago whimpered softly.

'It's all right,' Kathryn soothed, putting her arm across his shoulders as they climbed the stairs. 'Emma will make sure he doesn't get lonesome until you come back.'

Jon stopped short and stared at the huge array of every imaginable toy piled high in his room without a smile. There were cars and trucks of every size and colour, a miniature space station with robots and tiny spacemen sitting at the control centre. A tiny toy train was still in its huge box and a bright red two-wheel bicycle complete with training wheels stood in the middle of the clutter, its chrome fenders immaculate and shiny.

After a long moment Paul let out his breath harshly. 'Your enthusiasm overwhelms me, son.'

'Thank you, Uncle Paul,' the little boy said solemnly, holding on to Kathryn's hand. He made no move to touch any of the toys or games still in their boxes. His wide eyes lingered on the bike, but he didn't go near it.

'Think nothing of it,' Paul muttered through his teeth. 'Happy birthday anyway.' His tall body was rigid as he stalked past his brother standing silently in the doorway. 'You only think you've turned him away from me, Logan. But I'm not going to give up. Your turn's coming.'

'Don't threaten me,' said Logan with a cold smile. 'You'll only come out the loser.'

'That's been the story of my life up to now, hasn't it?' Paul flicked a speculative glance at Kathryn. 'But don't become too complacent, old boy. I have a feeling the tide's beginning to turn. I'm finally going to see you come out second best.' Then he left them, whistling softly as he made his way to his own room.

Kathryn heard this muttered exchange and looked sharply at Logan, but he avoided her eyes and spoke harshly.

'I want you to give Jon a bath before dinner,' he seethed. 'He'll be eating with us tonight, since it's his birthday. It'll be formal—Paul's not used to anything else. Emma said seven.' He roughly rubbed a hand over his jaw and let his gaze travel around the room crammed with toys before flinging himself out the door in disgust.

When he had disappeared down the hallway,

Jon turned to Kathryn. 'There's an awful lot of toys here, Mom.'

'I can't imagine what your uncle was thinking,' she agreed with an incredulous shake of her head. Even a five-year-old recognised a bribe when he saw one. 'We'll have to find a place to put them—but not now. Let's get you ready for your bath, shall we?'

As she watched him splash about in the water a few minutes later, her mind was churning wretchedly. She had to come up with some plausible excuse to miss dinner tonight. Formal, he had said. There was no way she could sit there in her hopelessly home-made clothes. Oh, why had she been so stubborn to refuse them in the first place? It was one thing to try to show Logan she didn't need anything from him, but now a horrifying realisation shattered through her: She had tried to hurt him. That was what it had really been. And in doing so, she only succeeded in hurting herself. She still had her pride, but it was cold comfort now.

Emma was waiting in the hallway outside the bathroom when Jon finished. 'I was going to put this in your room, dear, but it would probably get lost in the shuffle.' She held out a small tissue-wrapped parcel. 'It's not much, but I thought you'd like it.'

He hitched his towel tighter around his waist and accepted the package, eagerly tearing it open. An ice-blue mohair sweater lay within the folds of tissue paper, and he beamed with genuine pleasure before giving her a warm damp hug. 'Thank you. I love it! But when did you have time to make it?'

She smiled affectionately. 'Your mom's been such a big help with the house, I have lots of time to knit now. When your dad was little, I made him one too, but it took a lot longer then.'

'Can I wear it now? Please?'

'Of course you can,' said Kathryn, running her fingers gently across the soft sweater. 'Go and start getting dressed, darling, I'll be in to help in a minute.'

When he had left them she turned to Emma. 'When Jon's through I'll send him downstairs, but will you make my apologies to Logan and Paul? I've got a headache and I think I'll just take a long hot soak in the tub and then go to bed.' It wasn't original, but in her frame of mind it was the best she could do.

Emma was immediately all concern. 'I thought you looked a little peaked when you came home today. You go along to your room now. I'll see to Jon. Later I'll bring you a tray.'

'Oh, please don't bother. You've got enough to do without having anything extra added to it.'

'It's no trouble. I know headaches can be terrible things. Just go along,' Emma said briskly, 'and don't worry about a thing. I'll enjoy these few minutes with Jon.'

Kathryn gave her a small selfconscious smile and did as she was told. She hated having to lie, but there was no way she was going to sit at the dinner table tonight in that huge elegant room and be an embarrassment to her husband.

She stood at her bedroom window watching the lengthening shadows on the lawn turn darkly purple before jamming her hands in the pockets of her old blue robe. She had tried taking a soothing bath. Her hair was still piled on top of her head, but long black tendrils fell haphazardly about her pale face as her agitation increased. She felt so young and absurdly alone. If only she could go to Logan and explain things to him like an ordinary wife! But she wasn't, and he wasn't an ordinary husband. They were trapped in a marriage that was not a marriage with a child who was not their child. Or was he? She rubbed a hand across her eyes in despair. Now when she pictured Carol in the moonlight the scene was distorted. Who had been with her? Logan and Paul were so alike—and so different.

A gentle tap on her door stopped her whirling thoughts. Emma shouldn't have bothered, she sighed, crossing reluctantly to open it.

Logan stood in the hallway, dark and avenging in a midnight blue suit, frilled white shirt and impeccable blue tie, his hands on his hips, his face grim. 'You're keeping us waiting,' he said through his teeth.

Kathryn's face whitened, but she managed to keep her voice calm as she instinctively backed away from him. 'Didn't Emma tell you?'

'That you had a headache?'

She nodded mutely.

'Even I could think up a more original excuse than that, my dear wife. That one's a little overworked by women who can't face up to things. It's our son's birthday and I won't let you disappoint him. You've got five minutes to get dressed and come downstairs.'

She straightened her shoulders and lifted her head without flinching. 'No,' she said softly.

His expression hardened and his eyes took on the coldness of icy seas. 'Why not?'

'Please, Logan.' She turned her back to him and pressed her hands to her face. 'I just can't!'

His hands were bunched at his sides as he came to stand in front of her. 'It's your clothes, isn't it? Does Paul's opinion mean so much? How many meals have you shared with me without caring what you looked like?'

'It isn't that I didn't care,' she said helplessly. 'Oh, if only I could explain!'

'Try me.'

She took her hands away from her face. 'I——' she wavered, 'I just can't.'

Logan gave a short hard sigh and stepped to the built-in closet than ran the length of the room and flung open the doors on a dazzling assortment of brightly coloured clothing. There was everything here from evening gowns and daytime dresses to elegant pantsuits. On the floor, boxes were stacked containing shoes of every description. 'All you've got to do is put one on. Is that so hard to do?'

'Where did they come from? When——' Kathryn's throat closed on a choked whisper.

'I had them delivered this afternoon,' he said shortly. 'I knew you'd need them.'

'Delivered? This afternoon?' The blank look on her face was slowly replaced by a swiftly mounting anger as her eyes widened. Instead of being grateful for his thoughtfulness she felt an unreasoning resentment. 'And I suppose the delivery men were falling all over each other trying to bring in all the toys for Jon and all these clothes for me. It must have been a regular circus! No wonder Emma was practically beside herself when we came home!'

'Can't you just say thank you like any other wife and let it go at that?' Logan's jaw was tightly clenched and his face was full of white hot rage.

Hesitantly Kathryn walked to the closet and put a shaking hand on a bright green shimmer of silk. Her fingers involuntarily clenched the costly material. She needed clothes; he had provided them. She should have been grateful, but all she felt was a sharp sense of angry humiliation. No matter how much she hated to admit it, she had been bought. 'Thank—you,' she muttered reluctantly, trying to swallow back her pride.

His hands descended roughly on her shoulders, turning her to face him, and she couldn't help cowering away from the ferocity in his eyes. 'Like Paul said to Jon earlier, "Your enthusiasm overwhelms me". What's wrong with them?'

'Nothing.'

'Yes, there is. Tell me.'

'Please——' She tried to twist out of his grasp, but he held her closer.

'You think I've bought you, don't you? Go ahead and say it!'

'Yes,' she whispered defeatedly. 'I feel bought.'

She could see him shaking with rage. 'In order to buy there has to be an exchange of some kind. I paid for these things for you, but I don't expect a thing in return. They're simply a gift.'

'But so many? They're just like the toys Paul bought for Jon. Where's the difference?'

Blue ridges sprang out at the sides of his mouth and his eyes bored through her. 'Let's get something straight right now. Those toys for Jon weren't just birthday gifts from an uncle with no strings attached.'

'I know that. He's trying to buy Jon's affection, just as you're trying to buy me.'

'No, dammit! It's not the same. Can't you see?' Logan's fingers tightened on her shoulders. 'I'm not at all like Paul. I simply bought you these things because you need them. You know you do, yet you keep on refusing them. Why? Tell me!'

All at once his face was open. He really wanted to understand why she was fighting him. The sudden sting of tears burned the back of her eyes, forcing an unwilling admission from her.

'I'm trying to hang on to my pride—it's the only way. If I refuse the things your money can buy, you'll never own me. But it's not working out that way. I'm only making myself an embarrassment to you.'

Logan sighed defeatedly and dropped his hands to his sides. 'You're not an embarrassment to anybody. If you dressed in a burlap bag you'd be more beautiful than a hundred other women.' He rubbed the back of his neck warily. 'Change your mind. Accept the things I want to give you.'

'Oh, don't!' Kathryn turned away from him, pressing a clenched fist to her mouth. 'Why does it always have to be you giving me things? What can I give you?'

His face altered with sudden dawning comprehension and his voice took on a note of shock. 'I always thought you had pride, but I'm wrong.

It isn't pride. You have an inferiority complex. You don't think you're good enough to wear the clothes! And that's why you said you don't belong in this house, isn't it? You feel you're not good enough to be my wife!'

She turned back to him with a savage red stain on her face and neck, hating him for stripping away the thin veneer of false pride and exposing her gauche inexperience and unsophisticated vulnerability, but she straightened her shoulders and faced him without flinching. Her voice was a steady quiet whisper. 'That's right, Logan—I'm not good enough. I've never been good enough. It was always Carol. She was the one who fitted in, not me. You've both lived in a world I've never known. You've been to places, seen things, done things I've only dreamed about.'

'Carol again!' he exploded, gripping her shoulders in bruising hands. 'Do you think it mattered that she had poise and sophistication? That she knew which fork to use or which words to mouth? Things like that don't mean anything. It's what she *was* that counted. And she wasn't half the woman you are. Forget her!'

'Do you think I haven't tried? I look around this house, at all the things that fill it, and know I don't belong. Not the way Carol did.'

'Have I ever asked you to be something you're not?'

'Yes. You want me to dress in costly clothes and sit at your table as if I belong.'

Her head dipped forward in defeat, but he put his hand under her chin and roughly forced her to look at him. 'You do belong! I'm going to tell

you this only once and I don't ever want you to
forget it. I have money, a lot of it, but it doesn't
make me different from any other man. I use it
and I enjoy the things it can do—but you see,
money doesn't have me.'

Kathryn frowned at him.

'You don't see it, do you? That's the difference
between Paul and me. He's like my mother was—
and Carol too. No matter how much he has, it
isn't enough.' His hand made a wide sweeping
arc. 'My father built this house for my mother
according to her specifications. He furnished it
with the things that were important to her. It
took him a long time to realise that it still wasn't
enough.

'This is a long way from the one-room hovel
my father had in the Yukon, but he was happy
there as he was never happy here. Some winters
he was snowed in for months at a time and didn't
see a soul. But the Indians taught him how to
survive and he relished his solitude. He had no
family and had lived alone for years.

'Then he met my mother and wanted to marry
her, but she wouldn't have him because he had
no money.' The bitterness in his eyes stung her.
'He was a logger. That's all he wanted to be, but
she drove him, and money became his god too.
He could never get enough for her, there always
had to be more. She married him, finally, but I
don't think they were ever really happy. She
wanted more than he could give. When Paul and
I were born he thought he would have some
measure of contentment—but no, there still
wasn't enough money. She drove him to forsake

his integrity, to become blind to everything he believed in, all because money had her. Paul's that way. Carol was too. *I am not.* Can you see that?'

Kathryn looked at him. 'I know you've always worked for what you wanted,' she said slowly, haltingly.

'You're my wife, Kathryn. I work hard every day to provide for you and Jon. It's my salary we live on and it's never been handed to me. I'm not just handing it to you either. As my wife you're entitled to everything I work for.'

'But Paul? He said he was entitled to some money your father left.'

Logan turned away from her and stepped to the window where a blind black emptiness met him. 'Paul has an inheritance I won't let him touch only because he'd squander it all inside a year. He makes a great deal of money on his concerts. He could make more if he worked at it, but even that's not enough. Last year he came up with the idea that Jon is the key to unlimited wealth. If something happened to me, he thought he'd get custody of Jon and complete control of the Ramsey fortune. He started laying the groundwork, trying to ingratiate himself to Jon. Then all of a sudden he came up with this brainstorm that since he knew Carol before we were married, he just might be Jon's father. He's a very impatient man. He'll try anything to get Jon away from me just so he can have money.'

Her face whitened. 'This afternoon Paul told me he had an affair with Carol before you married her. He said Jon was the result of it. He was very convincing.'

Logan's whole body tensed. 'He had no right to say such a thing!'

'Is it true?' she whispered.

He stood absolutely still for a long screaming moment before he slowly turned from the window and stared at her. His jaw was jutting granite. 'What do you think?'

Kathryn didn't want to believe it had been Logan with Carol. She swallowed. 'Paul—Paul asked me to help him take Jon away from you.'

His face turned a sickly grey. His hands clenched at his sides. 'Can you imagine the kind of life Jon will have if you do? Paul doesn't want the boy; he wants the money he represents. Can't you see that? Carol was *my* wife. *I* married her, not Paul. Jon is *my* son.'

'But is he really yours? Were you Carol's— lover—before you married her?' she whispered, holding her breath, waiting.

Logan straightened his shoulders and braced himself. He looked as if he was struggling before coming to a painful decision, then with faint blue lines etched at the sides of his mouth he looked straight into her eyes and spoke with shuddering reluctance. 'Yes. Carol and I——' He breathed deeply. 'You know how beautiful she was. Can you blame me?'

Her eyes closed and she waited as the familiar stab of pain rushed through her. Then all her breath left her in a rush. 'No, I don't blame you, Logan.'

His mouth twisted as he walked to the closet.

His face was bitter, but he was once again completely in control. His voice was firm and implacable and cold. 'There's no way Paul can take Jon away from me short of kidnapping him. If you try to help him, you'll only end up getting hurt too. I swear I'll find him if I have to take apart the whole world brick by brick. Jon is mine. There's nothing you can do to change that.'

He ripped a dusty rose silk dress off a hanger and threw it carelessly in her direction. 'Wear this tonight,' he ordered without looking at her. 'It's Paul's favourite colour. You've got five minutes to get dressed and come downstairs. I'll wait outside the door.' Without giving her a chance to say a word, he left with a firm unhurried step and closed the door behind him much too quietly.

The dress was floor-length, draping loosely at the shoulders and softly gathered at the waist. Its colour was perfect for her, but for all the notice Logan took of her appearance when she left her room, she could just as well have been wearing her old jeans and T-shirt.

He took her elbow indifferently and kept his gaze straight ahead as they started down the stairs together. But halfway down Kathryn stopped and tilted her head, listening intently. A soft melancholy sound floated up to them, and it only took her a moment to realise it was Paul playing the piano. The music became louder, flowing in a great golden tide, and she was caught in its spell as the chords rose and swelled about them. Her heart began to beat in thick heavy strokes as something in the mournful melody touched an answering echo deep within her.

She wanted to turn to Logan and pour out an apology or an explanation—anything to end this mistrust between them, but one look at his profile twisted with cynical bitterness choked the words off in her throat.

He increased the pressure on her elbow, urging her down the stairs. 'Paul's exceptionally good tonight. Maybe he's using you as his latest inspiration,' he said in a sneering tone that grated.

There was nothing between her and Paul, but she didn't know how to convince him. 'Maybe he's just glad to be home,' she whispered.

'Home!' Logan pushed open the door that had been left slightly ajar. 'This is nothing but a big empty house. I doubt it'll ever be a home.'

Seated at the piano wearing a wine-red dinner jacket with a large froth of white lace at his shirt front and wrists, Paul was engrossed in his music and didn't see them come into the room. His head was thrown back and his eyes were closed as his fingers travelled over the keys with unerring swiftness. The music continued to flow in a mournful melody, and then suddenly it became stronger, wilder, with a tempestuous crashing discord. Paul opened his eyes and stood up abruptly in the sudden silence, pinning both of them with a slashing glance.

'Just look at this room!' he said in a shrill voice. 'Look at it!'

Kathryn tore her eyes away from him and made a quick sweep up and down the length of the huge room. A monstrous crystal chandelier was suspended from the centre of the ceiling and its brilliant prismatic light sparkled all the way to the ebony grand piano at the far end. There were open French doors that led to a patio now shrouded in darkness. Scattered antique tables and pale grey Queen Anne furniture flanked a large black marble fireplace, and on the floor was a wide Oriental rug with the predominant colours of muted oyster and green and blue. The walls were richly panelled in some light wood she couldn't name.

'What's wrong with it?' she whispered.

Logan allowed a slight smile to cross his face before he turned to her. 'Paul doesn't care for the changes we made. But I'd say it's quite an improvement.'

Paul threw them a look of undisguised loathing. 'Emma told me the Ming was broken! All the sculpture, the urns, the vases, the miniatures—everything that was here—is put away in boxes. Boxes! How could you? It's—it's a sacrilege!' he spluttered, sweeping his arms wide. 'This room was made for those things. You've even taken the Renoir off the wall!'

'It was time for a change,' Logan said quietly, keeping his voice calm. 'But if it bothers you so much, you're free to take all those things and leave. Find another place to house them. Nothing's stopping you.'

'You'd like me to go, wouldn't you?'

'Whether you go or stay doesn't matter,' Logan drawled before turning away.

'You don't fool me with your indifference, old boy,' sneered Paul in a goading voice. 'You know when I go I'm taking the boy with me.'

Logan stiffened, but his voice was deadly calm. 'The things in this house can go with you. The people stay.'

Paul flicked a glance at Kathryn, then looked back to his brother. 'What about your wife? Is she as obsessed with the boy as you are?'

'I can't speak for my wife—and I'll trust you to remember she is my wife—but Jon is my son. They both belong to me.'

'Well, well, well!' Paul smiled maliciously, and stepped away from the piano to a low cabinet where an array of bottles and glasses stood ready. He poured a measure of whisky for himself and took a long swallow before pouring a glass for Logan. 'Sherry?' he asked Kathryn.

She nodded because she thought it was expected of her.

'You're not so different from me after all, old boy,' he said as he slowly walked toward them, handing Logan the whisky and Kathryn a delicate crystal wine glass. 'I enjoy possessing things. With you, it's people.'

If he noticed the brief unreadable flicker crossing Logan's face, he didn't say anything. He was too busy enjoying his open mockery and his brother's inability to dispute what he said. Settling himself in an elegant wing chair, he crossed his legs delicately, waiting until Jon came to tell them Emma had dinner ready.

CHAPTER SEVEN

INDIGESTION had been the one thing Kathryn remembered most about Jon's birthday, and it was something she was becoming more familiar with as the week wore on. Paul had mentioned that his valet would be arriving the next day. What he didn't say was that he also expected his agent, his manager, hairdresser, personal assistant and secretary.

It was up to Kathryn to settle them in, but she didn't quite carry it off with aplomb. The house was big enough to accommodate all these men, but she was thoroughly intimidated when they all arrived at the same time and without even waiting to be introduced, began demanding, in the stentorian tones of Shakespearean actors, certain rooms and special diets as well as the deferential treatment befitting their artistic temperaments. Paul assured them his sister-in-law would see to everything since she was now the lady of the house, and with a pompous swagger, left her standing distractedly in the hall surrounded by tons of luggage.

Logan's lip curled as he watched them trail after Paul the same way Drago trailed after Jon, then he flicked a black eyebrow in her direction. 'You look surprised. Isn't this what you expected of a great concert pianist?'

Kathryn bit her lip, struggling not to let her

shattered nerves get the better of her, and
wondered how long they intended to stay.

'If it's any consolation to you,' his shoulders
flexed in irritation, 'this time next week they
might be gone.'

'With all this luggage? You mean they don't
intend to stay months?'

'They're like Paul. It's all part of an image.' He
watched her swallow hard and try to take it all in
her stride before his voice softened with com-
punction. 'They're just ordinary people, Kathryn.
Don't let them bother you. They work for Paul,
remember? But because he's so often in the
public eye, some of his notoriety has rubbed
off on them. It's given them swelled heads, but
they're no different from you or me.' He lifted
two of the heavier suitcases and gestured for her
to leave the rest. 'I've called a domestic agency
and some extra help should be starting tomorrow.
For tonight . . .' his shoulders lifted in a resigned
shrug, 'we'll just have to make the best of it.'

'You knew this was going to happen, didn't
you?' she asked with a trace of bewilderment.
'How can you let Paul disrupt everything like
this?'

'It's only once or twice a year now. If I let him
know it bothers me, he'll do it more often.'
Logan's face changed then and became cold and
hard. 'Besides, it's better to have him here where
I can see what he's up to and wait for his next
move.'

All the following week Logan didn't go to his
office but watched and waited at home. No
matter what Kathryn did or where she went, she

felt those icy blue eyes boring into her back. He might have said he wanted to keep an eye on Paul, but he made it obvious he didn't trust her an inch either. He kept in contact with his secretary by phone, and it was only after Jon was safely in bed each night that he would disappear into his study to tackle the mountain of paperwork waiting for him.

Paul was the only other one who knew what was going on, but he merely smirked and settled in more comfortably, and refused all his manager's attempts to interest him in another tour.

As one week turned into two, Margaret began stopping by in the early afternoons. Ostensibly, she was bringing papers she couldn't deal with alone or letters needing Logan's signature, but Kathryn felt a vicious stab of jealousy as she watched her make herself more and more at home. Paul invited her to stay to dinner that first evening and he was eagerly seconded by his manager and agent. She accepted at once, blending in with the rest of his ménage with astonishing ease, and now it was a nightly habit. Nothing and no one disconcerted Margaret, and Kathryn had to envy her.

It was only when Paul drew her aside and commented on how much time Margaret spent alone with Logan in his study after dinner that Kathryn realised what was happening. Before, Logan had had his moments of kindness to her even if he wasn't exactly trustful. But now that she thought about it, those moments were becoming all too rare. Margaret was usurping her position and she was letting her get away with it.

Logan had told her the morning after they were married that he wouldn't cross her barriers until she decided to take them down. Well, if she wanted him, now was the time. She had to let him know she was willing to be his wife in every sense of the world, and it wasn't going to be easy for her. Pride wasn't the easiest thing to swallow. She was afraid of making a fool of herself. What if he had got tired of waiting and decided he didn't want her any more?

After settling Jon that night, she restlessly paced the floor in her bedroom, trying to find the right words and alternating between hope and fear. Eventually the rest of the house became silent. She heard Paul's house guests retire to their rooms and the only ones left were Logan and Margaret closeted in his study. At midnight, she heard the front door close and the sound of Margaret's car on the drive, and taking her courage in both hands, she started down the stairs at once before it deserted her.

Logan was on his way back to his study when she made a slight sound behind him and turning, he scowled at her. 'What are you doing up?'

'Logan, I——' Her eyes could only lift as far as his shirt front and she twisted her hands together and felt herself stammering nervously. 'I—I'm sorry if I'm disturbing you, but I—wanted to talk to you.'

'Can't it wait? It's late and I'm tired.'

'Tired?' She looked up into his face and stiffened in ice-cold shock.

At the corner of his mouth was a bright red

slash of lipstick. Her stomach churned as she stared at it. The colour seemed to glow and grow brighter, shimmering and dancing before her eyes until she tore them away with an effort.

'I've had one hell of a day,' Logan said distractedly, dragging his hands through his hair before resting them at the back of his neck. 'There's trouble at one of the sawmills. I should have gone there rather than trying to handle it over the phone.' His dinner jacket had been discarded and his white frilled shirt was crushed and his dark tie was untied at his throat. A middle button on his shirt had come undone, and Kathryn's vivid imagination pictured just how that had been acomplished. She could almost see Maragaret's slender body pressed to Logan's powerful frame, her fingers seeking the warm wide expanse of his chest.

'That's—part of what I wanted to talk to you about,' she mumbled, looking everywhere but at him. Her fingers nervously pulled at the buttons on the front of her simple white dress.

'Now how would you know about the trouble I'm having?'

'I didn't—exactly—but,' she looked at the toes of his shoes, 'but I realise you can't neglect your business indefinitely. What I mean is——' She took a deep breath, her eyes darting nervously at the floor. Pain seemed to choke her throat. She couldn't tell him all the things she'd rehearsed. Not now. Not with his latest betrayal smeared all over his mouth. 'I just wanted you to know—you can trust, me, Logan. I wouldn't do anything to—to hurt Jon—or you.'

A black scowl deepened the rigid lines of his face. 'So, he's finally making his move,' he said in a voice almost too quiet, too controlled. 'What I don't understand is how you have the nerve to expect me to be taken in. You've decided to throw in your lot with him!' He towered in front of her, his solid body trembling with sudden rage. 'Why? What's he got that I haven't?'

Her face jerked up to his and her flashing eyes went instantly to that streak of red. 'You're wrong. There's nothing between Paul and me.'

'Do you think I'm blind? I saw the kiss you shared in the forest. God knows how many other times he's had you. And I've seen the way you look at him when you don't know I'm watching. You can't take your eyes off him!'

White-hot anger ran like a rod down her back, making her rigid. She forced herself to face him without flinching. 'He caught me by surprise in the forest,' she said stiffly. 'If you really saw what you were looking at you'd know I wasn't kissing him back. He only did it because he knew you were standing there and he wanted to make you jealous. Can't you see that? He hopes to come between us so it'll be easier for him to walk away with Jon. If I keep looking at him it's because I can't understand how someone could look so much like you yet be so different.'

'Keep your lies,' Logan grated through tightly clenched teeth. 'I don't trust you where Paul is concerned.'

'But you expect me to trust you with Margaret?' The question came rushing out unexpectedly in a voice choked with bitterness, and it sounded like an accusation.

'Margaret's got nothing to do with this!'

'Oh no? Then why did she leave her brand on your mouth?'

Logan ran the back of his hand across his mouth and looked chagrined when he saw the bright red lipstick. 'I can explain——'

'Oh, please! Spare me that at least.' Kathryn had to get out of here. A dull roaring started in her ears and bile was thick in her throat. Turning away, she groped blindly towards the stairs, sick with the irony of her timing. To think she had actually been going to offer herself to him tonight! She was his wife and she had no right to deny him. What a laugh! He was a normal healthy male. How could she think he was waiting patiently for her?

'Kathryn!' he called her, but she didn't hear him and he was forced to go after her. Gripping her by her shoulders, he pulled her back against his heated length.

The mist in her mind cleared at once and she struggled wildly. 'Don't touch me!' she shouted, suddenly catching the sultry fragrance of Margaret's perfume. It was all over him and it drove her mad. She jerked herself free and swung around to face him. 'How dare you?' Her breath was shallow and gasping as her body bent forward from the waist. Her fists clenched. 'You're no better than Paul!'

It was a mistake. As soon as she said Paul's name, she knew it was a mistake.

All the colour left his face at her look of

loathing. 'Kathryn.' He took a step towards her, but she fell back, never taking her stricken eyes off him. 'For God's sake!'

She started to turn away, but he reached out and caught at her wrists, swinging her around to face him. She resisted, bending backwards to loosen his grip, but he bent over her, holding her hands behind her, bringing his face close to hers. She swung her head from side to side frantically and her soft black hair brushed across his face. Its clean scent maddened him. The long white length of her throat was there before his eyes, holding him motionless for an instant, then his mouth helplessly fastened on the soft warm hollow. Her pulse pounded against his lips and he felt the silken flesh cling to them, warm and quivering and desirable.

All at once she became very still, her body seeming to have a will of its own, refusing to listen to the frantic demand she gave to be free. She was languid and weak, moulding herself to all the powerful angles and planes of his body. She felt the swelling pressure of her breasts thrusting against his shirt, the fragile bones of her wrists crushed in his hands, the softness of her thighs pressed intimately into the hardness of his.

A low groan deep in his throat suddenly brought her to wild life and she began to struggle in earnest before finally pulling herself away from him. Her eyes were a furious blaze of blue terror as she turned at once and ran towards the stairs without a word.

After a stunned second, Logan ran after her. She was already halfway up the stairs and he could see her long white legs flashing in the dim lamplight as she lifted her dress to keep from tripping on it. He lunged after her, trying to catch one of her ankles, but she was too fast for him.

Sprinting down the long hallway, she reached the safety of her bedroom and began to slam the door shut, when his hand flung out and held it. Struggling, they pushed it back and forth between them in a ridiculous battle. She could hear his noisy grunting breaths and the sound filled her with fear. Panic rose in her throat. She knew what he intended to do. The thought gave her an added strength as she thrust her shoulder against the door in one last effort to save herself.

But Logan was stronger and with a mighty heave, he crashed the door back on its hinges, throwing Kathryn back into the room. Her eyes were distended and wildly blue, never leaving his face as she awkardly picked herself up from the floor. Her heart was thumping madly in her throat.

He advanced slowly, his handsome mouth twisted. 'No better than Paul?' he grated.

He continued to come towards her, his eyes glazed and hard, his mouth a thin bluish line in his white face, his chest heaving with tortured gasps. 'You compare me to Paul? I've always tried to be a man of honour. But that's not what you really want, is it? Paul takes—and you women love it. You say I'm no better? All right, then, I won't be better! I'll take too. You, Kathryn. I'll take you.'

'No, please——'

He was on her, holding her still with one hand and using the other to grasp the neck of her dress and rip it down her body to her waist. Then his mouth was on hers, swallowing her hoarse cries as she struggled frantically, kicking and clawing at any part of him she could reach.

His hand tore at her bra, then cupped one warm small breast, his surprisingly gentle fingers closing over it making a quick gasping breath lodge in her throat. Stumbling, he pushed her towards the bed until she was against it, her knees bending from the pressure as she fell backwards. His body was heavy and heated and hard, his mouth still on hers, forcing it open in the shout of his desire, filling it with his warm moist breath. There was no stopping him. One knee slid between her legs, trying to force them apart, but the skirt of her dress was in the way.

In one last desperate attempt to free herself, her body arched instinctively, trying to fling him off. He dragged his mouth away from her and lifted his head to look at her, ravenous desire burning hotly in his eyes.

'You're mine, Kathryn. You're not saving it for Paul.'

'It's never been Paul,' she gasped, but he wasn't listening. Kneeling over her, he ripped open his shirt, sending the buttons scattering all over the bed. He pulled it out from the waistband of his pants and shrugged out of it and sent it sailing on to the floor. Little beads of moisture stood on his skin. His powerful muscles rippled in his chest and arms when he moved.

'Take off what's left of your clothes,' he

muttered, looking at the quivering whiteness of her body with open hunger.

Kathy trembled violently, unable to take her eyes off him, and embarrassment swirled through her mind and shame and utter humiliation in a hot suffocating wave. She wouldn't surrender to him. 'No, Logan. If you're going to rape me, I'm not making it easy for you.'

'Rape?' The word seemed to stop him cold. He loomed over her, still straddling her slender body but he didn't move. His eyes were deep and brilliantly blue as they searched her face. 'It won't be rape,' he said slowly.

Her throat constricted as she tried to control her shivering fear and the nervous chattering of her teeth. Her hands were at her sides, tightly clenched into the rich ivory silk bedspread. This was so different from what she imagined earlier. She had thought to find herself in bed with Logan, yes. But not like this! Never like this. Where was the love that was supposed to make it beautiful? This couldn't happen to her. Not without love.

She looked straight into his face and her eyes helplessly filled with huge wet tears that rolled down into her tangled hair.

For a long moment Logan simply knelt there looking at her. A spasm of pain crossed his face, then all the hard urgency of his body left him. 'Kathryn,' he said quietly. The sound was full of defeat. He knelt a moment longer, looking at her, then moved away.

He sat on the edge of the bed and dragged his hands through his hair, numbly looking about him. Most of his mother's things were gone. Kathryn had cleared the dressing table and all that lay on the shining surface was a plain brush and comb. All the rest of the small tables and chests and chairs had been removed, the crystal bottles and perfumes, the porcelain figurines and marble miniatures, all were gone. Logan looked at the unadorned ivory walls, the frothy white curtains billowing out from the windows, the uncluttered expanse of the pink and blue and gold Aubusson carpet. Now it was a gracious room, a room of a great lady of taste and delicacy.

He turned and looked at her again silently. She hadn't moved. Her eyes were closed and she lay very still and pale and quiet. Her dark hair fanned out behind her head like a black cloud. White lines sprang out at the sides of his mouth, and a look of deep suffering ran over his face when he saw what he had done to the front of her dress.

'I'm sorry, Kathryn,' he said humbly. 'I wouldn't blame you if you never spoke to me again.' A deep shudder ran through him as he stood up and pulled the edge of the bedspread over her in a protective movement. He watched her for a long time, seeing the way her throat kept forming little spasms as if she wanted to say something.

He hesitated, waiting, then a long sigh left his throat as he turned and picked up his ruined shirt and bent his head and silently left her, closing the door behind him.

Kathryn heard him go, but she couldn't move. It was a long time before she opened her eyes. By then the sky was turning faintly purple with the dawn.

CHAPTER EIGHT

THE sensation that all her safe and tidy world was suddenly falling to pieces all around her struck at Kathryn as she slowly showered and dressed that morning. All her actions were numbed and automatic, but her thoughts were churning. Nothing happened last night, she told herself. But it was a flagrant lie and she knew it. Logan had come close to raping her—yet he hadn't. He had stopped just in time. That was the thing to remember. No damage had been done. That wasn't strictly true and she knew she was just willing away the truth, refusing to accept it. A great deal of damage had been done. Before, there had been only the small barrier of her pride between them. Now, there was an insurmountable gulf of unforgivable hurt added to a misplaced jealousy and distrust. This had to be the end for them, yet where could she go? What could she do? How could she leave Jon?

She remembered the harsh feel of Logan's mouth draining hers, the heavy weight of his body, the rough yet gentle seeking hands, and a hot wave of shame ran over her. She remembered that brief moment when she had responded to him. If only she hadn't mentioned Paul! He was a miserable person who wasn't half the man his brother was. She pictured his smirking smiles and her mouth twisted. She had to get him to

leave here. Maybe then she could salvage
something of her life with Logan. Maybe then
they could talk about what happened—almost
happened—and forgive each other and go on
from there. But first she had to get rid of Paul.
He was at the root of all their problems, she was
sure of it.

She didn't know what she was going to say to
Logan when she saw him again, how she was
going to face him. But then she found she didn't
have to just yet. Jon came to her room with the
news that his father had gone to the office this
morning.

'Emma said there was some trouble at a
sawmill and he might not be back till late and
Uncle Paul said he'd teach me how to ride my
bike but I had to ask you first.' He said it all in a
rush and grinned up at her.

A breathless quiver ran over her and a sure
sense of calamity curled down her spine. Paul
wasn't wasting any time. She had to warn Jon to
be wary, but she wanted to do it in such a way
that wouldn't make him fearful. 'John——' She
hesitated, searching for the right words. 'You're
not—afraid—of your uncle any more, are you?'

'Oh no, Mom,' he said at once, smiling with a
shining innocence. 'Uncle Paul and I just had a talk
about that. Daddy's my father and he's my uncle.'

Kathryn's answering smile was troubled as she
searched his wide eyes. 'I'm glad, dear.' Her arms
went right around him, holding him close. 'But if
he ever says—anything that might—trouble you,
be sure to come to either your dad or me, all
right?'

'Sure, Mom. Can I ride my bike now?'

She nodded and watched him race away, but she was full of misgivings. She could understand why Logan hadn't stayed home today, but the swift way Paul had taken advantage of his absence made her uneasy.

Paul was just coming in the front door when she reached the hall and he held the door open for a minute, gesturing to her to come and look. 'Jon takes to that bicycle just the way I did when I was his age,' he said smugly. 'Logan wasn't half so daring then.'

Jon's face was flushed with triumph as he perched himself on the seat. His feet barely reached the pedals, but he didn't let that slow him down. He sped across the drive, leaning precariously to one side, balancing on the training wheels.

Paul smiled, then turned to openly study Kathryn's face. His flashing blue eyes fastened on a faint bruise on her neck. 'Did you manage to get any rest after your little tussle with Logan last night?' he asked callously.

Her lips parted as she sucked in a harsh breath. 'I—don't know what you mean.' She shuddered, her mind whirling.

'It's no secret, sister-in-law. Logan told me all about it. He's so full of remorse this morning. But that doesn't help now the deed's been done, does it? Ever the uncouth caveman, that's my brother. I must say, though, you don't look any the worse for wear.'

Hot colour flooded her face as she looked at him, totally at a loss. How could Logan tell *anybody*, least of all Paul? He stood there smirking at her and she wanted to scream, to reach out and claw at that handsome face so like Logan's, but she forced herself to hang on to her self-control and even managed to produce a tight smile to mask her humiliation. 'As you say, I'm no worse for the wear.' She forced the words through the hurt harshly gripping her throat.

'But, old girl,' Paul was all brotherly concern, 'you really shouldn't have fought him like that. It only forced him to run that much faster to Margaret. That's where he's gone, you know. I don't believe for one minute there's trouble at a sawmill. No, he's gone to Margaret. Now there's a woman who knows how to treat a man . . .'

Kathryn turned away, sickened. She didn't want to hear about Margaret.

But Paul followed her to the breakfast room where Jay Ravinsky, his agent, and Gerald Sawyer, his manager, were still reading the morning papers, their coffee cups empty on the table in front of them, and kept up his spiteful remarks. He knew what he was doing, and he also knew she had no weapons with which to fight back.

'Jay, I've been telling Kathryn here that she really shouldn't let Logan upset her. He's a brute, but he means well. What do you think?'

Kathryn stared at him aghast. Was what happened last night common knowledge?

Trying to be diplomatic, Jay Ravinsky shifted in his chair and folded his paper, then stood up as if preparing to leave. 'He was going on about some trouble at one of his sawmills this morning.

I expect it can be a worrying thing. Then too,' he looked pointedly at Paul, 'we've been here quite a bit longer than usual. Your brother probably feels, like I do, that it's time you began making plans for another tour. They've been begging us to come to Sydney for ages. How about it? You've had a prolonged rest. Australia should be pleasant at this time of year.'

Paul rubbed his hands together and pretended to consider the suggestion. 'Well, Gerald?' He lifted his shoulders gracefully and looked at the other man sitting at the table. 'Think you can arrange something, say, by the end of the week?'

The little man jumped to his feet and nearly ran from the room. 'It's as good as done,' he said abruptly.

Paul flicked an eyebrow to Kathryn and his mouth twisted. His voice held the barest trace of amusement. 'Poor Gerald, he never did like country living—too tame for him. That should make you feel better, old girl. By the weekend we'll be out of your hair.'

She should have felt relieved, but she couldn't shake the uneasy feeling that this was simply the beginning of the end of a carefully thought out plan to hurt—who? Logan? Jon? Herself? She didn't say anything but merely made an attempt at a small strained smile.

The day passed quietly enough, and Kathryn began to unwind as Jon abandoned his bicycle and played ball with Paul and Drago on the lawn behind the house. It was out of character for Paul, but she pushed away the disquieting thought and watched them. Maybe he was simply at a loose end too. It was that kind of day, warm and unusually sultry for late June. She sat barefoot in a lounger in a blue polka-dot blouse and white shorts, drifting in and out of the drugging mists of sleep. The breeze was gently cool, ruffling through her hair, and she could hear the mesmerising hum of bees somewhere near and smell the resinous scent of pine. She had been watching Paul with Jon, but another picture kept superimposing itself on her mind. Logan was there, looking achingly handsome in jeans and a bright white T-shirt. Jon was dressed the same way. Then there were several other children in playclothes with them, another little boy and two little girls with pink ribbons threaded through their long dark hair.

They all were laughing and they kept calling Logan 'Daddy,' and once, when he lunged for the ball, it eluded him and he lost his balance and sprawled flat on his back in the grass. Immediately they flung themselves on top of him and began tickling him, their giggles high and shrieking and piercing.

Jon kept beckoning Kathryn to come and join them, but her legs were weighted down so she couldn't move. When she reached down to find what was holding her, she saw a man's hands tight around her ankles. Paul's hands. And then his face was there, mocking, grinning, telling her he couldn't let her go to Logan. 'He doesn't want you,' he kept saying. 'He wants Margaret.' And sure enough, when she looked back to where Logan was sitting on the grass with his children around him, she saw Margaret float out to him, her gold cap of blonde hair like a halo around her head. She kissed him gently, many times, and left a trail of bright red lipstick all over his face . . .

'*Kathryn!*'

She woke with a start and looked straight into a pair of incredibly blue eyes, so warm and welcoming it made her heart pound. 'Logan——'

He drew in his breath sharply and something flickered in his eyes, then they moved slowly and consideringly over her flushed face. 'Having a nightmare, old girl?' Paul queried with a chilling little curl to his lips.

'Oh!' She turned her head away, trying to get her bearings, nervously wiping at the surprising tears that had matted her lashes together. She should have known it wasn't Logan. He wasn't speaking to her any more. 'I—I must have dozed off.'

'That must have been some dream, the way you were twisting and moaning!'

She blushed a vivid red. 'I don't remember.'

'It was about Logan, wasn't it?' he insisted. 'Even after last night you still love him!'

Kathryn hunched her shoulders and shifted uncomfortably. He was leaning over her, resting his hands on either side of her head, his face close to hers, and she felt trapped. The sun had gone down and now the breeze was decidedly chilly.

'Tell me,' he said cruelly.

'Please, Paul——'

'He's got it all, hasn't he? How can you still love him after last night?' His mouth twisted as he straightened. 'Have you no pride? Let him go. It's Margaret he really wants.'

Kathryn blinked rapidly, wondering how much of this was a dream and how much reality. 'No, that's not true.'

'He loves her, has done since she started working for him. He realised what a mistake it was to marry you, but he doesn't know how to get out of it.'

'I don't believe you,' she choked. 'Logan wouldn't say such things to you.'

'You'd be surprised what he tells me. In all those years he spent searching for you, he built up an image of you in his mind, but now he knows he was wrong. You're not the woman he thought you were. Let him go, Kathryn. Don't wait for him to ask you to leave.'

She became very still, searching his open face. It *had* been a mistake. She *had* failed Logan. She wasn't the woman she had been five years ago. Maybe it was only his stubbornness and affronted pride that made him keep searching for her and finally marry her. The hand she dragged across her eyes was cold and clammy, jerking in a frightened gesture. All these thoughts had been resolutely pushed to the back of her mind ever since she had come here. She couldn't take them out now for Paul to see. She looked past him to the empty lawn. 'Where's Jon?' she asked.

'*Jon?*' he exploded. 'Is that all you have to say? Where's Jon?' His face became a mottled red. 'You're a fool, do you know that! A fool!'

She stared at him for a long minute then with a sudden flare of suspicion said very quietly: 'Where is he, Paul?'

His lips twisted. 'Emma called him for supper.'

'Already?' She shook her head in a daze. 'What time is it?'

He glanced at his gold watch, then lifted his shoulders. 'Almost seven-thirty.'

Gathering herself together with difficulty, she got up from the lounger and smoothed her tangled hair, trying not to look as dishevelled as she felt. 'I don't know how I could have slept so long,' she muttered. 'Is Logan home yet?'

'Er——' Paul pretended to be embarrassed, 'Margaret phoned a little while ago. He's been—detained. Personally I think he just can't face you after last night. There was this strange music in the background——'

'Oh!' With a little sob, Kathryn broke away from him and ran to the house. She had to get away from him. He was making her see things she wasn't ready to face yet.

Firmly shutting her bedroom door, she sank down on her bed with a small choking cry. Her head was throbbing painfully and her confused emotions coupled with that persistent feeling of apprehension made her physically sick. She had to laugh because she was afraid if she let herself cry she'd never stop. She never should have let herself doze off like that. The nightmare she had had was bad enough, but now real life was beginning to take on the same stark qualities. Everything was falling down around her ears, and there was no way to stop it.

She gave a groan and forced herself to get up and run a hot bath, a normal thing to bring back normalcy to her life. After she thought about it, she knew Paul was wrong. Logan didn't love

Margaret. He loved her. He had said so a number of times. Last night was simply a—lapse—on his part. He had been a man driven to the edge of his control. She couldn't blame him for that. And those were her children she had seen with him on the lawn. They had dark hair, didn't they? Not blonde. Paul wasn't going to stop her from being a part of that family. She'd take a long hot soak and dress in her finest dress and wait for her husband. No matter how long it took, she would wait, and they would talk things out and start to rebuild their relationship.

When her bath had filled, she crossed the hall to say goodnight to Jon and apologise for not being in sooner.

He was lying on top of his blankets in just his underwear, and she frowned at him.

'It's too hot for pyjamas,' he said quickly before she could say anything. Then he turned his back to her. 'Goodnight, Mom.' His tone was brusque and he didn't kiss her as he usually did.

That vague apprehension curled down Kathryn's spine again, flaring into the full-scale knowledge that something was definitely wrong. 'Is everything all right, darling?' she asked, gently rubbing his shoulder.

He shrugged her hand away. 'Yes, Mom. Goodnight.'

'Jon——'

But he clearly didn't want to listen. He hunched his shoulders and burrowed his face further into his pillow.

Feeling rebuffed, Kathryn stood and watched

him for a long minute, then quietly turned away with pain in her eyes.

Back in the bathroom she mulled it over. That wasn't at all like him. Something had to be wrong. Or was it only her own heightened emotions making mountains out of molehills? Jon was entitled to his own irritable moods once in a while too. Heaven knew there were enough undercurrents running through this house for the past several weeks to make anyone uncomfortable!

Stepping out of the bath, she wound a thick white towel around herself and then loosened the pins holding her hair and brushed it vigorously. She took her time choosing what to wear, pulling out dress after dress and discarding them one after another. Then she found it—a rich shimmering knee-length gown of cream-coloured satin, it had a daring halter neck. She let it drift over her head, then smoothed the clinging circular skirt and turned to look at herself in the mirror.

It was elegant and sophisticated, and with her hair loose and flowing in a midnight cloud to the middle of her bare back, there was no doubt she was all woman. She had never worn anything like this before, never displayed her body so daringly. The thrusting curves of her breasts were boldly hinted at without actually exposing them, but the dress left little to the imagination, clinging as it did to her curving waist and hips and thighs. For just a moment she thought it might be too provocative, too sensuous, but then she told herself this was what was needed tonight if she

was to compete with Margaret. Besides, Logan
had chosen this dress for her. She clung to that
fact, and her face softened when she thought of
him going to all this trouble for her. She had
never thanked him properly—but that would be
taken care of tonight. Everything would be out in
the open. So many things would be put right.
Paul was leaving soon and they would have the
chance to start over.

Driven by restlessness, she stepped to the long
windows and stood looking out to the lawn
below, trying to remain calm. Everything was
quiet now except for the low murmuring of tree
frogs and crickets. A soft warm breeze was
blowing from the distant mountains, bringing
with it a melancholy sound as it whispered
through the dark green pines in the forest. Her
face lifted in that direction now and a thin shiver
ran down her spine. There was no good reason
for this uneasiness, but she couldn't shake it off.

Her evening meal was a solitary one. Emma had
told her Paul and the rest of his friends had gone
into town to finalise the arrangements for their
Australian tour. Kathryn sat alone in the vast
dining room under the soft light of a crystal
chandelier. A maid came in and served the meal in
silence, then just as silently withdrew. Kathryn
looked down the length of the table, fingering the
lace cloth and heavy silver and crystal and china,
and felt apprehensive and slightly lost. Would she
ever learn to take this for granted the way Logan
did?

By the time she had finished picking at her
food, she was almost numb with tension,

wondering how she was going to begin to tell
Logan all the things that needed to be said. Her
eyes kept darting nervously to the door and every
footfall made her think he had finally come
home.

'Is the meal that bad, Kathryn?' Emma asked
quietly, coming to clear the dishes. 'You've
mangled that roll until I have to wonder why you
bothered to take it in the first place.'

Kathryn looked at the shredded pile of bread
on her plate and flushed guiltily. 'I'm sorry,
Emma, I don't know what's the matter with me.
I——' She lifted her shoulders helplessly. 'Have
you heard from Logan?'

Emma shook her head. 'Sorry, love. Would
you like some more coffee? Maybe that'll settle
you.' Her face softened with sympathy. 'It takes a
little getting used to, doesn't it? Being on your
own again, I mean. Those men certainly do
demand attention. I for one will be glad when
they've gone.'

'I was always a solitary person, so it's not really
a hardship. I like being alone,' Kathryn said
quietly, knowing it might have been true once
but not any longer. Jon had wound his way
around her heart, Logan too, and now she missed
them both. 'Er—no coffee, thanks.' Nervously
preoccupied, she pushed her still half full cup
away. 'I think I'll just go and check on Jon again.
He complained about being too warm earlier.'

'I hope he's not coming down with something,'
Emma frowned. 'I thought he was acting a little
strange at supper. He wanted to wake you, but
Paul said you probably needed the rest because

you didn't sleep too well last night. That seemed to upset him.'

'Oh, I wish he had,' said Kathryn. 'I feel guilty for not putting him to bed myself.' She shot a painful smile at her and quickly left the room. That apprehension was stronger now, running up and down her spine with a sudden urgency.

At the bottom of the stairway she paused and took herself to task. It was ridiculous to jump to conclusions. She was working herself up for nothing. If she went up there she might only be disturbing Jon unnecessarily. But all at once she had the strongest feeling that Jon needed her, and running her sweating hands nervously down the sides of her dress, she hurried to his room.

Everything was dark and still as she pushed open his door. It took a minute to adjust her eyes to the gloom—then her heart began to pound in thick heavy strokes when she saw his bed was empty.

A thousand things ran through her mind: He'd run away. Paul had taken him. Logan would blame her. Jon was hurt, lost, even now he might be calling for her . . .

Her heart rose in her throat and stuck there. She stood alone in the darkness, totally bereft, the taste of blood in her mouth.

CHAPTER NINE

AFTER a minute her frantic terror began to subside. Jon couldn't have gone far. There wasn't time, for one thing. He probably was just in the bathroom and she was wildly jumping to conclusions.

Forcing all her misgivings to the back of her mind, she went looking for him, calling his name in a clear steady voice. He wasn't in the bathroom—or in any of the bedrooms on the second floor. She methodically searched every one and panic was beginning to set in again when she reached the kitchen and found Emma and Mr Higgins, Paul's valet, relaxing over a cup of tea.

'Have you seen Jon?' she asked, trying not to sound hysterical.

Emma looked astounded, then concerned. 'He's not in his bed?'

'No, and I've searched all the other bedrooms. He's not *anywhere*!'

The always correct Mr Higgins got to his feet and hurriedly slipped on his dark jacket, deeply conscious of having been caught enjoying himself. He was a tall man with a mass of grey hair and deep laugh lines at the corners of his eyes. 'Now, now, Mrs Ramsey, you know what young boys are. He's probably just playing a joke on you. When did you last see him?'

Kathryn bit her lip and took a deep calming

breath. 'About an hour and a half ago.' Her voice wobbled. 'He didn't have his pyjamas on and when I started to ask him about it, he cut me off saying it was too warm. Something's wrong—I just know it!'

'Hmmm.' He remained unruffled and stepped to the screen door, peering out at the blackness. 'It is a warm night. He simply might have gone out for some air.' Quietly pushing open the door, he stepped outside.

Kathryn hesitated, hating to voice her suspicions, but they came out anyway. 'Paul,' she said with low uncertainty. Her face was strained and she put a clenched hand to her mouth feeling a suffocating wave of fear rushing over her. 'You don't think he—took him, do you, Emma?'

'Took him? Took Jon?' Emma gasped, but almost at once recovered herself. 'No, Kathryn. I know what you're thinking. I know the jealousy between the two boys and the talk about who's really Jon's father, but I'm sure Paul had already gone out with his friends before you last talked to Jon.'

Mr Higgins came back then. 'Can't see a thing,' he said with a shake of his head, 'but I know someone with a much keener sense of sight and smell.' He walked over to the small cage where Drago had been penned for the night.

'Of course!' Emma smiled with relief. 'He follows Jon everywhere. He'll know in a minute where he's gone.'

The minute his cage was opened he bounded to the door, whimpering excitedly, scratching to be let outside.

'Do you have a torch, Emma?' Mr Higgins asked.

She rummaged through a drawer at the sink and found a flashlight and handed it to him.

He looked at Kathryn. 'All right, Mrs Ramsey, open the door. I'll keep this trained on him and we'll see where he goes.'

They all watched as Drago made a beeline straight for the woods.

'*No!*' Kathryn gasped. 'Jon can't have gone there! We don't allow it in the daytime. It's so dark now, he'll be lost for sure!'

'Shall I ring Logan?' Emma touched her arm lightly. 'If anyone knows those woods like the back of his hand, it's Logan.'

'No!' Kathryn breathed deeply, taking the flashlight from Mr Higgins' unresisting grip. 'Don't do that just yet,' she amended apologetically. 'We don't know for sure he's out there and we'd just be upsetting Logan for nothing.' She swallowed past the huge dry lump in her throat and fought for composure. Then all at once a sudden calmness began to seep through her, a certainty, and all her fear left her. A slow simmering anger took its place. Jon was out there, all right, and somehow Paul was behind it. That was why he went into town tonight instead of letting the others make all the arrangements themselves. She couldn't say anything yet because Mr Higgins owed Paul his loyalty and Emma did too, to a certain extent. This was something she would have to do by herself. She would find Jon first and bring him back, then she would have it out with Paul.

'I'll see if I can follow Drago,' she said. 'In the meantime, will you search the rest of the house? Just in case?'

'Oh, Kathryn, it might not be safe out there.' Emma started to protest, but when she saw the stubborn set of her jaw she took a different tack. 'At least let Thomas go with you.'

Mr Higgins was standing there stiffly and she could almost hear his heels click together. 'Of course, Mrs Ramsey. You really shouldn't go alone.' He didn't look as if he'd relish the job, but he was ready to do his duty.

'No, it's all right,' she said calmly. 'Someone needs to be here in case he comes back before I do. If you'll just search the cellars—maybe the attic . . .'

He nodded, trying not to look relieved. 'If you're quite sure.'

She gave him a small strained smile, then swung around abruptly and pushed open the door.

The moon was full and she had no difficulty picking her way across the lawn. The forest loomed closer with the suffocating blackness of a shroud and she almost lost her nerve. Her legs turned to water and her breathing came fast and laboured. How could Jon have come out here? Maybe more importantly, why? Switching on the flashlight, she swung the beam through the trees, listening intently for the least little sound. '*Jon!*' she shouted. '*Can you hear me?*' Her heart banged against her ribs at the answering silence. '*Jon!*'

Thinking only of him, she plunged into the wood, looking back over her shoulder to get her

bearings and make sure she didn't lose sight of
the house and get lost herself. Peering again into
the blackness ahead of her, she walked straight
into a tree and staggered to her knees. Her hair
caught on a low hanging branch and sharp spiky
limbs stabbed against her face and uncovered
arms, making them sting, but she wouldn't let
herself stop and go back for help. The over-
powering scent of pine, thick and rotting, made
her long for a breath of clean air, but she had to
go on. Her son was in here somewhere. Maybe
Drago had already found him and was waiting for
her. The darkness was oppressive and she had to
fight her imagination as well as the maze of trees
blocking her way. Her toe caught on a fallen log
and she nearly lost her footing as something
scurried away in the darkness. A strangled yelp
came from her throat and the light swung crazily
in her nerveless fingers. Several birds noisily
fluttered their feathers resenting her intrusion
into their late night haunt, and an owl hooted
eerily. Kathryn gulped. Her jaw trembled and
her mouth shook.

'*Jon!*' she cried desperately, trying not to be
afraid of the stealthy rustlings all around her. In
daylight she probably wouldn't even notice them,
but the darkness made everything so much more
menacing. '*Jon! Please answer me!*' Oh God, if he
was hurt she'd never forgive herself. It was her
fault he was out here. She never should have
fallen asleep this afternoon and left him alone
with Paul. There was no telling what he might
have said to make him come out here like this.

She thought of the animals that sometimes

were seen in the area, deer and elk and bear, and her expanding imagination had them all converging in a circle, ready to pounce on her helpless son, their ferocious grinning jaws wet and gaping and full of sharp pointed teeth. '*Jon!*' Her voice was choked with panic and sounded unnaturally high and shireking as it echoed back to her.

She knew that with the denseness of the trees the sound of her voice might not carry, but as she stopped to listen for an answer in the ringing silence, she could hear the low gurgling of the stream twisting through the wood. Maybe Jon would be able to hear her after all. But that comforting thought was shortlived. It suddenly brought an added fear. What if he had fallen into the water and drowned?

'*Jon! Are you all right? Answer me! Jon!*' What if he was lying hurt somewhere and couldn't answer? Her heart hammered wildly in her throat, but she forced herself to breathe deeply to calm herself. Panic wouldn't help anything. Her panting breaths became whimpers of futility. Methodically sweeping the beam of light through the darkness and picking her way around thick tree trunks, she startled several small animals, their eyes glowing eerily in the light before darting away. Rats? she thought wildly. Did rats live in a forest? Oh God! She stumbled and barely managed to keep from sprawling face forward on the ground. Staring straight ahead, she held her breath, catching her lower lip between her teeth, trying not to cry.

The darkness and the rustling silence seemed to press down on her until she was a trembling mass of nerves. Her eyes were wide and blindly peering, straining to see through the thick impenetrable wall of pine trees. A thin film of cold sweat stood out on her brow and upper lip and her hands clenched around the flashlight. She wanted to scream and run as fast and as far as she could, but like her nightmare earlier, her ankles seemed weighted down and her legs curiously boneless. She had to force herself to keep picking her way forward, keep putting one stumbling foot in front of the other. She couldn't stop, not now. She had to find Jon. For a moment she was overcome with a formless, voiceless grief. Stopping abruptly, she closed her eyes and tried to swallow past the fear clutching at her throat and cutting off her breath. Jon's trusting face rose up before her. He needed her and she couldn't get to him.

A cold breeze began to blow and it sliced right through her, making her shiver. She should have stopped to put on a sweater. Her mouth twisted and shook and a travesty of a sob rattled in her throat. She wasn't dressed for tramping in the woods. Her heels were too high, her dress too elegant, her hair too loose, so it caught on every low-hanging branch no matter how far down she tried to duck. One of her shoes slipped off her foot, so she kicked the other one off too and left them behind and went on barefoot, oblivious to the rough prickling of pine needles on the bottom of her feet, shredding her pantyhose.

How could this have happened? How could she have allowed it? Jon must be scared to death. He was only five, too small to be out here alone.

Why? Why? The question banged in her head like a broken record. What could Paul have told him to make him come to the woods at night?

She tried not to think of what Logan would say, but his face rose before her and she could see the angry condemnation written all over him. 'So, I could trust you, eh?' she heard his sarcasm clearly. 'You and my brother planned this. The minute I let Jon out of my sight he gets lost in the woods at night. It's no coincidence!' His eyes would flash a deep and bitter blue, the lines at the sides of his mouth would be white and harshly rigid. He'd never forgive her. She'd never forgive herself.

'*Jon? Can you hear me? Please, please answer me!*' Her voice was getting hoarse as her desperation increased. She had to find him. Glancing over her shoulder again to make sure the lights of the house were still behind her, she jerked to a dead stop. They were gone. Only darkness met her frantically searching gaze. Nothing but complete, empty, black, silent darkness. Her eyes darted back and forth, left and right. No matter which way she looked, the lights were gone. That, added to all the terrors of the night-time forest, robbed her of the last vestige of self-control. It was her undoing. She was lost now as well as Jon. Despondency washed over her and, completely unstrung, she sank to her knees, the flashlight rolling drunkenly out of her hands. Sobbing hysterically, she buried her face in her arms and fell full length on the ground, her tears flowing fast and free and burning like bitter acid.

She had failed. Failed. Failed! It repeated agonisedly over and over in her head. Jon needed her. He was out here somewhere and she failed him.

Then all at once her heart plunged to a sudden stop and an icy fear clutched at her throat, skidding over her skin with cold wet fingers as she heard something approach, creeping stealthily on the thick carpet of pine needles. She felt the warm moistness of a panting breath near her shoulder and wanted to scream, but even as her mouth opened and a terrified gasp rose from her lungs, sheer horror closed her throat and no sound could emerge.

A high-pitched whimpering cut through her strangling fear, and Drago let out a short sharp bark and put his paws on her arm and tried to lick her face.

Shaking uncontrollably, all her breath left her in a rush as she lay stunned, blinking in disbelief, then she shot to her knees and reached for his solid warmth, clutching at him for dear life. 'Drago!' Half sobbing, half laughing, she clung to him. 'Where's Jon?'

His short quick barks echoed through the darkness and it took her a few minutes to loosen the death grip she had on him.

'Oh, Drago, where's Jon?' He barked again, and suddenly Kathryn knew Jon was very near. She was certain of it. Most likely he could see her in the dim watery beam of the flashlight lying on the ground near her, but for some reason, he wasn't coming to her.

'Jon,' she said softly, 'I know you're here. Are you all right?'

Her heart thumped madly. He could hear, but he wasn't answering. She just knew it. But why? *Why?* It had to be Paul—something he had said. For some reason Jon wasn't supposed to let her find him. He was hiding from her!

'Jon,' she said, the tears so thick in her throat they made her voice wobble desperately, 'do you remember when I first came here? That first morning I met you?' She waited. Her voice died away in the silence. 'You told me if I ever got lost you'd find me. Jon, I'm lost now. I don't know how to get home, which way to go. And I'm afraid. Please help me, Jon. I *need* you!'

A sudden rustle behind her made her heart stop, and then Jon was running to her, flinging himself into her arms.

For long minutes they held each other, Kathryn's body absorbing the deep racking shudders of his, her soft incoherent murmurs soothing his anguished sobs, her arms tightening protectively around him giving as well as taking comfort from him.

'Oh, Jon! Jon! We're lost, but we're together— that's the main thing. Are you all right?'

His little head bobbed up and down under her chin. He was shaking, shivering with cold as he buried his face in the thin folds of her dress. He wore jeans and a thin cotton shirt and his skin was ice cold to the touch.

'Why, Jon? Can you tell me why you came out here?' The question wasn't accusing; she simply had to know.

He tried to burrow deeper into her body and didn't say anything.

Still kneeling, she held him for long minutes, her arms wrapped tightly around him, then gently eased back into a sitting position on the ground with him in her lap. 'I'm not angry, darling,' she said soothingly, trying to choose her words with care. 'I just can't imagine what would bring you out here at this time of night. Won't you tell me?'

He shook his head and refused to loosen his choking hold on her.

'It's Uncle Paul, isn't it?' Kathryn kept her voice steady with an effort. 'He said something to you today, something that made you come out here. Please, Jon—I have to know what it was!'

The silence stretched for ever. Kathryn felt the little boy's whole body clenched with tension, but she waited. However long it took, she meant to find out why.

Just when she was sure he wasn't going to answer, he sagged against her and all the stiffness drained out of him. His voice was a dry breathless rustle.

'Uncle Paul told me—there was a way I could prove I wasn't his son,' he said softly, shuddering again. 'Daddy loves the forest. If I came out here and—stayed all night——' he gulped and squeezed his eyes tightly shut, '—then—then that would mean—I'm not Uncle Paul's. I'm Daddy's.'

'Oh, Jon!' Her heart went out to him. She felt a tight dry ache in her throat, a burning pressure at the back of her eyes, and for a second there was an awful impulse to burst into tears. How could Paul do that to him? An adult would find it hard to stay here alone at night. How could he expect a five-year-old child to do it? 'He was wrong, Jon,' she said fiercely. 'Staying out here doesn't prove you're Daddy's son. It only proves you're a brave boy—very brave. But I already know that, and so did your daddy.' She clung to him, her voice hardening with sharp cold anger. 'You'll never again have to prove you're Logan Ramsey's son. If Paul wants proof, I'll be the one to give it to him, not you. Carol was my sister. I knew her better than anybody. I'll have a talk with him and that will be the end of it.' There was a bitter twist to her mouth. She closed her eyes and saw again that silvery body entwined with her sister's. It was galling to have to tell Paul she had actually seen them, but if it put an end to Jon's harassment it would be worth any amount of humiliation.

She looked at Jon and hugged him tightly. 'That is, I'll tell him if we ever find our way out of here!'

He smiled a white watery smile. 'Drago knows the way.' He reached out to the dog curled up beside him and stroked behind his ears. 'Let's go home, Drago,' he said softly.

Kathryn had her doubts that he really knew the way but there was no other choice. She had to follow where he led.

The way out of the woods was just as tortuous as the way in. Her heart pounded unevenly as she stumbled behind them. Jon held tightly to her hand and kept encouraging her as she skirted past vicious pine branches. Smiling in spite of her misgivings, she realised he was seriously taking care of her.

'Don't worry, Mom,' he reassured her over and over. 'Drago knows where he's going.' Then he pointed straight ahead. 'See?'

The glimmer of lights through the trees made her widened eyes swim. 'Oh, darling, I never would have made it without you!' Relief swept through her, almost making her collapse. They'd made it after all. She hated to think what Logan would have to say. He must be home by now, waiting for her, probably furious.

Stumbling, they picked their way out of the thick trees and started across the lawn, meeting Emma half way.

'Jon!' she cried. 'She found you! Are you all right?'

'My mom was lost,' he said with quiet dignity. 'She needed me and I found her.'

Emma looked at Kathryn over his head and her mouth twisted, taking in her cuts and scratches and a long tear in the side of her dress. 'No one's home yet,' she said softly.

Kathryn's breath was unsteady. She tried to control the helpless shaking of her body, but her voice wobbled on the edge of hysteria. 'Then will you help me get Jon to bed?'

At once, Emma was brisk and efficient, taking charge without taking over. She listened while Kathryn bathed him and her mouth thinned as she realised she was glossing over Paul's ruthlessness, telling her why Jon had gone out there.

When Jon was again settled for the night, he

smiled up at both women and murmured a sleepy 'Goodnight' before turning over and promptly falling deeply asleep.

Emma watched him for a minute, then turned to Kathryn. 'If you don't mind, I'd like to stay here tonight, in case he wakes up or has a nightmare. I've got some knitting I want to finish anyway and I'm sure you've got some things you want to finish with Paul. I think I heard him come home a few minutes ago.'

CHAPTER TEN

KATHRYN didn't linger in the shower. Washing away the dirt and soot, she looked ruefully at the long angry scratches on her arms and legs, then threw on a pair of jeans and a long-sleeved white blouse and dragged a brush through her hair, wishing she could get rid of Paul as easily as she could get rid of the pine needles in it.

Paul was playing the piano. She heard him as she descended the stairs and she stood for a moment in the hallway outside the door, fighting for control. It wouldn't do to burst in on him, ranting and raving like an outraged mother. She had to remain calm and keep her dignity if nothing else. Forcing back her violent anger and grief and pain, she shuddered, lifting her head, listening as a long rolling chord rushed at her like approaching thunder. It was a discordant sound, wild and leaping, and it struck her into a poised calmness.

He was unusually bad this evening, as he had been on many other evenings, only she had never realised it before. What he was playing couldn't be called music. The mechanical precision was there, but the heart and soul necessary to make it live was not. It was an empty echo of a composer's dream, and she wondered if Paul was aware of it. If she recognised this about him, surely other people who knew music, who attended his concerts, must know it too. Maybe that was why he needed the money Jon represented. Maybe he couldn't get first-class bookings any more.

A sudden disconcerting pity for him came welling up, but she crushed it back at once. She didn't want to pity him. He deserved her hatred and anger for what he had done to Jon, not her compassion because he was so lacking in musical genius.

Taking a deep breath, she pushed the door open and gave the room a cursory glance. It was empty except for Paul—which was just as well. She didn't think she could stand it if she had to wait any longer to confront him.

Her steps were rapid and jerky, taking her straight to the piano where Paul sat lost in his wild, toneless noise. He wore black slacks and a white frilled shirt with lace at the collar and cuffs. His eyes were closed, his face twisted and bitter. Never had he looked less like Logan. Kathryn stood without moving, and when he opened his eyes, his fingers jammed the keys and stopped abruptly, making the silence ringing between them thick and heavy.

Paul must have seen something in her eyes, because all at once he jerked his hands to his chest and held them there as if afraid she might slam the lid on them. It was an exaggerated movement, and all it did was deepen her anger.

A choking sound of anguish rattled in her throat and scorn dripped from her. 'How dare you?' Huge wet tears stood in her eyes, but she managed to keep her voice even. A restrained manner meant dignity. She wouldn't lose hers now. 'How *dare* you?' she said again, quietly.

He blinked uncertainly, then blustered: 'What are you talking about?'

'Oh, you know what I'm talking about, Paul. But it didn't work. I went after Jon and found him in the forest and now he's asleep upstairs. Safe in his bed. And Emma's with him. We agree he has to be protected from you.'

All the colour left his face and his jaw started to sag, but he stiffened at once, his eyes darting impulsively past her. He wetted his lips and dragged his gaze back to her again as if suddenly cornered. 'I'm sure I don't know what you mean. He's my son—why should he be protected from me?'

'Don't you dare call him your son!' she shrieked. Her control slipped, the breath in her throat rattled harshly and her eyes were terrible. 'You're the last person in the world to call yourself a father! No father would deliberately confuse his son. No father would deliberately destroy his son's faith in the only man he's known in that capacity merely for spite.' Her hands curled into white fists on the edge of the piano and her whole body clenched as she leaned forward closer to him. 'No father would deliberately ask his son to spend a night alone in the woods to prove he's his son!'

Paul's jerky breathing filled the room. Jealousy and anger and fear ran through him as he stared at her. 'There has to be some way to prove he's mine. I've got to have him.'

'No! You don't want him for himself. It's the

money he represents—the bloody Ramsey fortune! You don't care about him as a person. You'll never get near him again, not as long as I'm living in this house!'

'You can't stop me.'

A dull red colour ran into her face and she swallowed, controlling herself with difficulty. She didn't want to have to tell him, to have to expose her humiliation and affronted pride to his view but she had no choice. 'But I can, Paul. You're wasting your time trying to convince anyone he's your son. I've always known he wasn't.' A searing pain ran through her, holding her rigid. 'Why do you think I left Logan all those years ago? Why I disappeared without a trace? He betrayed me, Paul. I saw him—with Carol. There was no doubt it was him. They were—so—passionate——' She squeezed her eyes shut and shuddered helplessly. 'He couldn't refuse what Carol offered, no man could. I saw them together—on the very day he proposed to me. He had to have one last fling, and Jon was the result of it.'

Paul's eyes widened and he seemed to shrivel. 'What?' he whispered in outrage. 'Carol told me he never touched her.'

'Do you think she wasn't above lying?' said Kathryn in a slow voice, seeing again that haunting silvery picture. 'I saw them, and I couldn't stand it. Logan had betrayed all the love I had for him, so I left. I should have realised I was too tame for a man like him. I think all along I did know, but I was young then and full of illusions.' Her voice was a whisper, and Paul's face blurred before her eyes.

'The swine,' he muttered, rising from the piano bench, but Kathryn blinked away the sting of tears and impaled him with the blue flash of anger in her eyes.

'Yes, he's a swine, Paul. But no more than you are. At least I was a grown woman. You tried to hurt an innocent child, and I'll never forgive you for that!'

'But, Kathryn——'

'Don't you "but Kathryn" me!' She was livid, shaking, wanting to rake her nails down his face. Her voice wobbled, but she held it steady with a tremendous effort. 'It's done, Paul. It's over. Finished. We both know Jon is Logan's son, and as long as I'm married to him, he's my son too. You'll never get near enough to hurt him again.'

'All right, so he's not my son. I had my doubts, but it was worth a try. You don't have to make such a big production out of it. You sound as if you're trying to throw me out of my own house!' Paul was indignant, ignoring the angry tears sparkling on her lashes and the tight compression of her mouth.

'That's exactly what I'm doing, Paul. I want you out of here—now, tonight. And take all your friends with you. I'm sick to death of them!'

He gaped at her. 'You have no right to say such a thing!'

'I have every right. I'm Mrs Logan Ramsey and this is my home now. There's nothing here for you any more.'

He looked at her as if he couldn't believe his ears.

Kathryn stared back at him without moving,

hoping he couldn't see how her mind was churning. Maybe it was wrong to throw her weight around like this. She might not be Mrs Logan Ramsey for very much longer, but Paul didn't need to know that. By the time Logan had installed Margaret here as his wife, Paul would safely be on the other side of the world, and that would give Jon time to get over the trauma without worrying about Paul. 'Logan's given you all the things from this house that matter to you. And you have your music. You could make a lot of money with it if you'd work at putting some feeling into it.'

Paul's face changed and he looked astounded, then angry. 'What do you know about music?' he sneered. 'You have no appreciation of it. You don't know Chopin from Tchaikovsky!'

'No, I don't,' Kathryn admitted, her smile really just a convulsive movement of her mouth. 'But I've heard you practising day after day. You're technically perfect, I'm sure, but there's always something missing, isn't there? Something even a person without an ear for music can hear. There's no—feeling, no power, no—emotion.'

Paul stood up slowly, like an old man, staring blindly through her, full of an anger too terrible for words. 'You don't know what you're saying,' he whispered. But there was no conviction behind it and both of them knew it.

'You spend so much energy hating your brother,' she said quietly, again struck by an unwilling compassion for him. 'Just think what it could sound like if you channelled that into your music.'

He stood at the piano and his wide shoulders sagged. He held out his hands, looking at the long sensitive fingers, staring at them for a long moment before clenching them into powerful fists and crashing them down on the keys. 'It's always Logan, isn't it? He's got everything I ever wanted: money and power and position. He's got feeling and emotion and he doesn't have to be afraid to show it. He's never had to please anybody but himself to get it. He doesn't have to worry about an adoring public who change loyalties at the drop of a hat when some new virtuoso comes on the scene.' His eyes slid to hers and after a moment his mouth twisted into a hateful smile and he laughed mirthlessly. The smile abruptly vanished as he looked to some point behind her and his lip curled. 'But maybe he hasn't got it all,' he said softly in a meditative voice. 'He never really wanted those things. All he ever wanted was you. But he can't have you, can he? You hate him too.'

Kathryn began to shiver, the stricken blue of her eyes the only colour in her face as she lifted it regally and lied through her teeth. 'That's right, Paul. He betrayed me—he and Carol. No one can expect me to forgive him for that.'

His head snapped back, releasing something in him, and he flushed with pleasure. 'Once someone hurts you, it's impossible to forgive him. I'm glad you realise that.'

She knew what he was trying to do. In an unsubtle way he was telling her never to forgive Logan. He couldn't know her love was such that she would forgive him anything, over and over,

endlessly. Her whole body quivered and she tried
to stiffen her spine so he wouldn't see it. She
smiled, a painful silky smile that didn't reach her
eyes. He needed to believe there would be no
happiness for Logan. That was the only way he
would leave and stay away for any length of time.
'That's right,' she said. 'And you hurt me too,
Paul, by hurting Jon. I'll never forgive you for
that.'

Her expression disturbed him, the sick
whiteness of her skin and the thin blue line of
her mouth, the way she was holding herself so
stiffly, but he smiled back, refusing to take her
seriously.

'I mean it, Paul. You're not welcome in this
house any more—for as long as I live here.'

His eyes again darted past her, narrowing
on something, and his hands clenched at his
sides. 'You're not really throwing me out?' he
gasped.

'Let's say I'm asking you to leave,' Kathryn
said coldly. 'I want you gone before Logan comes
home tonight.'

'But—but——' His face whitened and he began
to stammer.

'If you go now, I won't tell Logan what you
did to Jon.' Her voice was high and strained and
she knew she couldn't take much more of this.
She was exhausted, drained, her control was
almost gone, her nerves stretched to their limit.
'Now, Paul. Please, go now.'

He knew he was beaten, but he wasn't a good
loser. His face twisted into a sneer. 'All right, I'm
going. As you say, there's nothing here for me

any more. But don't think your threat is making me leave. Logan and I came home together. He already knows.' His eyes blazed, then he roughly pushed past her and started for the door.

A frown started to crease her forehead, but as she turned, her whole body clenched with a violent sickening lurch and it was wiped right off her face. Logan had been sitting behind them all the time, in a wing chair, listening to everything.

Her chin lifted at once in a proud and fearless gesture that was purely instinctive. Shards of ice ran down her spine, making her whole body tingle and the hair at the back of her neck stand on end. She was utterly defenceless. Something was slowly coming unravelled deep inside her and there was no way to stop it.

This was the end for them, then. He had to have heard everything she said with such conviction—her lies to Paul, her condemnation of himself, the way she kept saying she would never forgive him. There was no way to begin to explain now.

She closed her eyes in despair. Logan deserved to be free of her, free to find a woman who could love him completely, the way he was meant to be loved, someone who trusted him, and once that trust was given, never to withdraw it no matter what she thought she saw.

Carol hadn't lied to Paul when she said Logan had never touched her. Kathryn knew it without a doubt, without the slightest uncertainty now. It wasn't Logan with Carol in the moonlight. Now she could see it without blinkers, now that it was too late. Logan wouldn't have done that to her. He loved her. He had always loved her. But she hadn't loved him enough to trust him, to go to him and tell him what she had seen and ask him to explain. All the jagged pieces of the puzzle relentlessly fell into place.

He hadn't rejected her all those years ago by taking what Carol offered. Kathryn had rejected him. She had been such a coward, so afraid to face the truth, so afraid to let herself be loved.

That was all it was. He was Logan Ramsey, a strong, powerful, wealthy man, better in her eyes than anyone else in every way, so far above her. She couldn't believe he could love an insignificant person like herself, so in a moment of self-preservation she had jumped at the first chance to leave him. And now that she knew what love was all about, that rich or poor, love was a total commitment to selfless giving, it was too late.

She opened her eyes and watched him slowly rise to his feet and come towards her without haste. He looked as if he hadn't slept in days. He was pale and drawn, with lines of exhaustion etched at the sides of his mouth and eyes that were curiously bleak. His navy blue business suit was crushed and wrinkled. The vital blackness of his hair stood out as if he had been dragging his hands through it.

She started to tremble, her stomach fluttering nervously as he advanced, and a sense of panic gripped her. More than anything she wanted to fling herself into his arms and beg his forgiveness, but if she so much as touched him she knew she would break down, screaming, in front of him.

He stopped within an arm's length of her and stood looking into her distended eyes silently, without moving. Tall and lean and disruptively attractive, he seemed content just to stand there, his unreadable eyes moving from her stricken face to the shallow rise and fall of her breasts beneath the white blouse, lingering there a moment before travelling up again and narrowing on her trembling lips.

'You *saw* me with Carol?' he said, his mouth shaking as if the words were forced from him.

Kathryn hesitated. 'I saw Paul with Carol.' Her voice broke on a sob.

Logan couldn't help himself. His expression changed to one of blazing anger and his chilling blue eyes swept her face. 'Then—why?'

'Why what?'

'*Kathryn,*' he grated, his hands roughly clamping on her shoulders as if he wanted to shake her until her teeth rattled. 'Why did you condemn me? If you knew it was Paul, why did you leave me? Why?'

She gazed at him with tremulous eyes. 'I didn't know it wasn't you. Not then.'

The anger left his face and was replaced by a fleeting incredulity. He snatched his hands away from her as if burned. 'When did you—begin—to have doubts?' he said unevenly.

'When—when I saw Paul for the first time. I knew you had a brother, but I didn't know you were a twin! You never told me. I couldn't believe it. And then I—I thought I might have been mistaken. It must have been him, not you.'

'But you weren't sure? Even then? You thought I could do that to you?' Logan spoke rapidly, through clenched teeth, coming closer to her quivering body so her face was a mere breath away from his. 'You thought I could betray the love we had in such a way?'

His face was contorted with bitter loathing, and Kathryn could only move her head helplessly from side to side as tears welled up in her eyes. 'I'm sorry, Logan,' she whispered. 'I didn't know.'

'You're *sorry*! You *didn't know*! What kind of empty words are those? Do you think by saying them that justifies what you did, what I had to go through searching for you all over the world for five miserable years? You're *sorry*?'

His eyes blazed such cold blue fire it had to melt the ice choking her heart. She shuddered into stillness, bereft and angry, and looked at him with a grim, cold dignity.

'I won't ask for your forgiveness, then, Logan.' Her voice throbbed and she stiffly backed away from him. 'It's so easy for you to stand here condemning me, isn't it? You're so righteous. Go ahead and despise me—it's all I deserve. But while you're at it, just remember you didn't trust me either. When I asked you if you'd been Carol's lover before you married her, all you had to do was tell me you weren't. But you couldn't trust me with the truth, could you? You were afraid to tell me Jon wasn't your son. You expected me to betray you.'

A spasm of pain crossed his face as he stood looking down at her, and all at once it suffused with the dull red blood of shame. He trembled, and without thinking, his arms lifted in an imploring gesture.

Kathryn took another step backwards, and after a defeated moment his hands dropped lifelessly to his sides.

'You're right, Kathryn.' His jaw hardened and his mouth moved in a grimace that was meant to be a smile. 'I wouldn't accept your apology, but here I am, wanting you to accept mine. Isn't that a laugh?' He looked at her distractedly. 'But, *God*, I really am sorry!'

She remembered the last time he had said that to her. Had it been only last night? It seemed a lifetime ago. She could tell he suddenly remembered it too by his haunted, agonised expression. Then his eyes closed and his breath became ragged and he buried his face in his hands.

'You must hate me,' he whispered.

Kathryn was appalled. 'Hate you?' Her head moved from side to side in a tremulous denial. 'No, Logan, I don't hate you. I wish I could—it might make it easier for me. I thought I hated you once, all those years ago, and then I wondered if I ever really loved you. The only thing I've ever been sure of is that you loved me.'

Logan slowly dropped his hands, his eyes holding hers silently for a long minute before taking a hesitant step towards her, his face ghostly white. 'Oh *Kathryn*! I do love you!' His voice broke and she suddenly found herself caught up in his crushing embrace, her head pressed savagely against his shoulder, his fingers helplessly bunched in the tangled black cloud of her hair. She could hear his heart racing in his chest and feel its throbbing against her temple. He lifted her tear-wet face to his and trembled. 'My Kathryn!' He tried to smile, but with a helpless exclamation his lips fastened on hers, clinging, prising open her mouth, losing himself in her sweetness. His hard body curved around hers as if he would absorb her into himself completely.

And every nerve in her body clamoured in passionate answer to his silent questions. She was his. She had always been his. Her heart hammered in her throat and drummed in her ears. Her arms slid around his waist as a wild sweet urgency ran through her. Mindlessly, her fingers dug into the rippling muscles of his back. He was real, he was here, he was hers!

She never knew how long they stood like that, but she willingly would have given anything to make it last for ever. When eventually Logan loosened his grip and let her draw a little away, still within the circle of his arms, she was panting and breathless. 'I thought I'd lost you,' she whispered shakenly. 'The things I said to Paul— and last night——'

'Paul's known that about his music for years now. He needed to hear it from you, a virtual stranger. Maybe now he'll work on it. As for last night—I'll spend the rest of my life making it up to you. Oh God, Kathryn!' He rested his forehead against hers and tightened his arms.

'You were right—it would have been rape. I never thought I was capable of such a thing.'

'You weren't, Logan. When it came right down to it, you couldn't hurt me.' Her face changed. 'It never was Paul. You believe that, don't you?'

'I heard the way you threw him out of here.' He shrugged his wide shoulders helplessly. 'I have to believe it.'

A brilliant red ran into her face. 'I know it was presumptuous of me. I had no right to throw him out of his own house, but I couldn't help myself. I was so furious. He tried to hurt Jon——' She broke off, shuddering, and Logan held her closer.

'He expected Jon to spend the night in the forest?'

She nodded, her hair brushing against his face. 'He told him, since you love it so much, if he could stay there the night, alone, without being afraid, that would prove he was your son once and for all.' She buried her face in his chest and clung to him, remembering. 'He's just a little boy, Logan. And to ask him to do such a thing——'

'You went after him and you found him and brought him back to me. That's all you have to remember. Forget the rest.' Logan cupped his hands around her face, his long fingers disappearing in her hair, and his eyes blazed a deep burning blue as they roamed over it. 'You didn't have to think twice about going after him, I'm sure. You knew he'd be terrified—as you must have been. Only a real mother would have done that.' The harshness and strain left his face and a white smile softened his features. 'And now

Paul's gone, but you'll still be right there, ready to protect Jon from all the other things waiting to threaten him. You're his mother.'

'And you're his father,' she said with a quickening breath. 'I convinced Paul.'

'You convinced me!'

Her shoulders lifted and a tremulous smile came and went. 'When I'm angry, I tend to react without thinking.'

'So I've noticed.'

She knew he was thinking about the way she had left him without a word all those years ago, and her face flamed as she looked him full in the face. 'I've said and done so many stupid things. Can you ever forgive me?'

'What's to forgive, Kathryn? I love you. That's all there is.'

'You can still say that—after—after the way I misjudged you? First with Carol and then— Margaret——' She let the name hang in the air between them.

'I had no choice with Carol,' he said softly. 'She was pregnant with Paul's child and there was no way he could marry her. She came to me and demanded help. Since you'd disappeared so completely, I did the only thing I could do. I married her and gave her the Ramsey name. But I never touched her, Kathryn—not once. Since the day you promised to marry me, there's never been another woman. Margaret tried, I'll admit that, but I wasn't even tempted. I chose you a long time ago, and I've never regretted that choice.' He smiled and his eyes held hers, then with the utmost mendacity he said: 'I knew you loved me—even when you wouldn't let me near you. I just needed the patience to wait until you were ready.'

Unexpectedly Kathryn's eyes filled with tears. 'I don't deserve that. I've been so stupid and blind and proud. I ruined everything.'

'Nothing's ruined, my love.' His mouth moved against her hair and when he felt her quivering, he wrapped his arms around her and held her in the warm secure circle. 'It's all just beginning.' His lips trailed over the long curve of her neck and teased the line of her jaw with seductive mastery before letting her move to fully return his kiss.

Her toes barely touched the floor as she arched against him, her mouth finding his with hungry passion. Her hands were resting on his chest and somehow his shirt buttons became unfastened and her fingers mindlessly slipped beneath the material and dug into the damp, burning warmth of his skin. A flicker of wild forbidden excitement ran through her. She remembered the silken feeling from last night and she suddenly wanted to lie naked with him and feel the length of his flesh against every inch of hers.

'You once promised to love me, Kathryn,' Logan said shakily. 'It's there again in your eyes and I can feel it in the pounding of your heart. Will you be my wife and let me love you the way you were meant to be loved?'

She shuddered with ultimate longing. The past was truly gone. All the mistrust might never have happened. It was a new beginning, as he said. 'Oh, my darling,' she said against his lips, 'I promise to love you all the days of my life.' She turned and pulled him blindly towards the stairway before he impatiently swept her up into his arms, desire blazing in his laughing eyes. 'And a promise is for ever.'

Take these 4 best-selling novels FREE

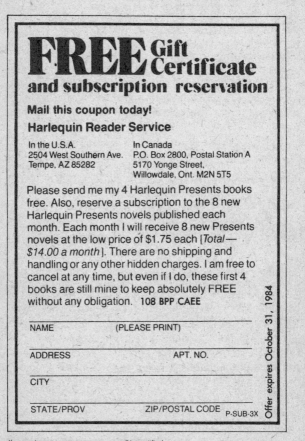

Yours FREE, with a home subscription to HARLEQUIN SUPERROMANCE.™

Now you never have to miss reading the newest HARLEQUIN SUPERROMANCES... because they'll be delivered right to your door.

Start with your **FREE** LOVE BEYOND DESIRE. You'll be enthralled by this powerful love story...from the moment Robin meets the dark, handsome Carlos and finds herself involved in the jealousies, bitterness and secret passions of the Lopez family. Where her own forbidden love threatens to shatter her life.

Your **FREE** LOVE BEYOND DESIRE is only the beginning. A subscription to **HARLEQUIN SUPERROMANCE** lets you look forward to a long love affair. Month after month, you'll receive four love stories of heroic dimension. Novels that will involve you in spellbinding intrigue, forbidden love and fiery passions.

You'll begin this series of sensuous, exciting contemporary novels...written by some of the top romance novelists of the day...with four every month.

And this big value...each novel, almost 400 pages of compelling reading...is yours for only $2.50 a book. Hours of entertainment every month for so little. Far less than a first-run movie or pay-TV. Newly published novels, with beautifully illustrated covers, filled with page after page of delicious escape into a world of romantic love...delivered right to your home.